GOODEY'S LAST STAND

JOE GOODEY MYSTERIES (BOOK 1)

CHARLES ALVERSON

WATCHFIRE
PRESS

Published by Watchfire Press.

Watchfire Press

www.watchfirepress.com

www.watchfirepress.com/alverson

Cover design by Kit Foster

www.kitfosterdesign.com

Goodey's Last Stand/Charles Alverson. – 1st ed.

Print ISBN: 978-1-940708-11-9

ISBN: 9781940708102

ALSO BY CHARLES ALVERSON

Caleb

The Word

Goodey's Last Stand (A Joe Goodey Mystery)

Not Sleeping, Just Dead (A Joe Goodey Mystery)

Fighting Back

Mad Dog Brewster

Apache Dreaming

Imagine Me

Hooligans

The Triple Shot Box (3 Crime Novels)

The Coming of Age Box (3 YA Novels)

For a current list of titles and further information, please visit
watchfirepress.com/alverson.

GET A FREE SHORT STORY COLLECTION

To instantly download **Ryan's Way and Other Stories** completely for free, sign-up for Charles Alverson's author newsletter at watchfirepress.com/alverson.

1

I STIFF-ARMED MY WAY THROUGH A DARKENED SIDE EXIT of San Francisco General Hospital. Outside, the post-midnight sky was rare. It was a night to bring joy to the hearts of lovers, astronomers, and insomniacs, but all I could see was a narrow strip in front of me down the pocked concrete steps where I was supposed to put my feet. Behind me in a private room a nearly dead bank vice president lay draining pus and keeping his own counsel despite my forty-three hours of sleepless investigation. Ahead of me was the parking lot, my car and, I hoped, a large chunk of unbroken sleep in my own lumpy bed.

With my eyes more closed than open, I let gravity pull me down the short flight of steps. But just as my right foot touched the bottom step, a sharp explosion like a small-caliber gunshot went off in one of the dark recesses of the big, dirty-brick hospital. Automatically I dropped the remaining step into a crouch behind the thick concrete railpost. My .38 service revolver was in my hand.

"Hey!" I said, too tired to think of anything original. "Police. Drop it and come out slowly."

Whoever it was didn't say anything, but I could see him, dimly, against a black wall. And then the glint of a high parking-lot light bounced off something brightly metallic moving about where his hands had to be.

I pulled the trigger just once, and an elderly night watchman with an unlit, aluminum flashlight in his hand fell to the dirty blacktop bleeding profusely. In tiny shards all around him were the remains of the light bulb he'd dropped.

2

"It's no fucking good, Joe." Ralph Lehman, the chief of detectives and my boss, a great tackle of a man ground down by nearly thirty years of nit-picking detail, looked across his desk at me. His big, football-shaped head with its sparse hair rested at an acute angle on the back of a massive leather chair.

"I know," I said. I still hadn't been to bed, although it was now late morning, and I felt like a bagful of carpet fuzz. "I know." I sat across from Lehman on a rickety wooden chair, trying not to slump.

"It's bad enough," he went on wearily, "you've got to shoot a poor, defenseless Polish immigrant working nights to put his son through dental college. An old duffer who can't even speak English, who's hardly been off the boat fifteen minutes. Who doesn't need the second belly button you gave him."

I opened my mouth but couldn't even get out another "I know."

"That's bad enough," Lehman said, "but I suppose you know who that old Polack was."

"Is," I said. "No was. Is. He's still alive. Hell, he's not even hurt very badly. He probably feels better right now than I do."

"Is, then," Ralphie said. "I repeat: I suppose you know who that poor, miserable, suffering old bastard is?"

"Yes," I sighed. "I know. Whiteside told me, Brennan told me, Hokanson told me. Even that hot-pants secretary of yours told me as I came in here this morning. The mayor's uncle."

"No, his cousin. His thirteenth, twice-removed, once-canonized cousin. Distant, I will grant you, but nonetheless Sanford F. Kolchik's mother-loving cousin. And do you know who vouched for the old fart to come to this great land of opportunity and violence?"

"Sanford F. Kolchik?" I hazarded a guess.

"Correct," Lehman said. "The very same gentleman of proud Polish extraction who's been on that telephone there no less than four times already this morning, demanding your head on a coal shovel. And that was between calls coming down from Rabbit Ears' office. At one time I had Sanford F. and Rabbit Ears on the phone at the same time. And they both wanted the same thing."

"Blood?"

"Right again. And not just anybody's." Lehman picked up a mucous-colored file folder from the near corner of his desk top. I recognized it as a police personnel file and didn't have to guess whose. I think I must be psychic. Especially after fifty hours without sleep.

"The full treatment, eh?" I said.

"Fuller than you think, Joe-boy," Lehman said. "Hizzoner wants you hit with the overloaded boat: attempted murder, assault with a deadly weapon, malicious wounding, drunk on duty, lurking with intent to mope and maybe even dirty pocket handkerchief."

"Is that all?"

"Probably not. He and his high-ranking brother are together right now trying to figure out some way to get you crucified with dull and rusty nails."

"What have they got against me?" I asked. "All right, I used to bump heads with The Brother when he was still human. But I hardly know Sanford F."

"What did you have against their cousin?"

"I get your point. But what's the upshot of all this? I see you've got my personnel jacket there. I'm not up for promotion, am I?"

"Not exactly, Joe," Ralph said. "I get the feeling that you don't appreciate the gravity of the situation. The brothers Kolchik think you're down in the cells right now with last night's crop of drunks. If they knew you were sitting there mocking the afflictions of their punctured relation, you wouldn't be the only one who's through. And I want that pension next year. I've earned it."

"Through? Did you say through?"

"Through," he said with depressing finality as he opened the long folder. "Positively thuh-roo." Lehman rifled through the loose papers like a gambler trying to plant the ace of diamonds. He looked up at me. "You know, Joe," he said, "you're not exactly Mr. SFPD."

"What about the citations?" I countered.

He ignored my question. "It's thirteen years now, isn't it, Joe?"

"You've got the date right in front of you," I said. "It'll be fifteen years on October thirteenth—my birthday."

Lehman let that pass. "This thing with Mrs. Stanfield was a real winner," he said, singling out a modest sheaf of papers.

"Mrs. Stanfield," I said, "is a malicious, petty, small-minded, overweening, foul-mouthed drunk."

"You're right. But she's also the wife of Superior Court

Justice Moses Stanfield, a deplorably powerful man in this city."

"That's where I made my mistake," I admitted.

"That's where you made your mistake," he agreed. "A mistake that would have gotten anybody else slammed back into uniform on the coldest beat on the piers." He looked at me compassionately. "Joe, do you know why you were made a plainclothes detective after only three years on the force?"

"My citations," I said proudly. "It says right there—"

Ralph cut me off with a hand like a first-baseman's glove.

"Joe, they're very nice citations. They're wonderful citations. Stopping that break at the County Courthouse was the best day's work you did in your life. But the reason—the main reason—you got yanked out of that baggy serge uniform, Joe, is that you don't look like a policeman."

Lehman's eyes flicked up to see how I was taking this supreme insult. When it looked as though I wouldn't crumble, he went on. "You don't even look like a rent-a-cop. If only you knew the number of calls we used to get from citizens complaining about somebody impersonating a policeman. And it usually turned out to be you."

"All right," I said, "so I'm not the Nordic ideal. I never asked to pose for recruiting posters. I've gotten along okay for almost fifteen years. My citations..."

"Your citations," Lehman said, taking half a dozen sheets of paper from my file. "I'm going to take your precious citations upstairs and beat Kolchik and The Brother over the head with them and pray that they don't disintegrate. But first you've got to sign this." He flipped a sheet of paper around with his forefinger and flicked it across his desk at me.

"Sign what?" I asked, bending low to catch the gliding sheet of stationery through a mist of fatigue. I read the first typed line aloud: "I, Jonah Webster Goodey, do hereby tender my resignation as..." I looked up at Lehman. "Resignation? Ralph—"

"Sign it, Joe," he said, almost pleading. "Use your head. It's the only way to save yourself and maybe me too. Kolchik doesn't want your resignation. He wants your balls. Both of them. Your only out is to sign that piece of paper and quietly disappear."

"Disappear?" I asked. "And do what? Chief, I've been a cop since I came out of the army, since I was twenty-one lousy years old. I may not be much of a cop, but it's all I know." And I meant it. Even seen through my fond eyes, Joe Goodey was not a clever, versatile man.

"Take up a new career," said Lehman. "Thirty-five's not old. You went to San Francisco State, didn't you?"

"For two and a half years," I said. "Ten years ago. At night. All I learned you could stuff inside The Brother's ear and have room left for his brain. I've got maybe forty-seven credits to my name, and most of them are in anti-insomnia sessions like 'You and Your Society.' Ralph, I'm not an educated man. I'll starve to death. Kolchik will see to that."

Lehman grunted as he leaned over his broad desk and took a black plastic pen from a flat holder. He extended it toward me like a cyanide pill. "Joe," he said mildly, "you've never fucked me up personally, and you're not a bad guy, so I'm going to give you an incredible break."

"What's that?" I asked. "An ex-copper's funeral after they find my withered body in some fleabag down on Mission Street? Thanks." Ralph looked at me sadly. Or maybe it was just tiredly.

"Joe," he said, "I'm a bit hurt. I really am. We go back a long way, you and I. I mean, both on the force and outside it. I'm trying to help you." I believed him. I didn't want to, but I did. We did go back a long way. More than ten years before, I'd come fairly close to becoming his son-in-law until his daughter Mary got smart and married a chemical engineer. And through the years it had been Lehman who'd gotten me out of more jackpots than I liked to think about. His support had gotten me through the Stanfield incident. Maybe he was trying to help me again. I was too tired to know.

"Okay, Ralph," I said. "You're right. I'm an ungrateful bastard. What's the deal?"

"Joe," he said, "if you sign this resignation and leave San Francisco—today—for at least six months, I'll see that you get a private operative's license if—when—you come back. Then you can make a living anyway. There's always work for a private op in this town."

"A private operative?" I sneered. "I hate those bastards. If they're not gigolos, they're stoolies. Or both. And the best ones are crooks. I respect even political cops like Kolchik's brother more than a lousy private detective."

"Joe," said Lehman, "I hate to say this, but you look like a private dick. It's a natural. I'm surprised I didn't think of it before."

"Thanks."

"Are you going to sign?"

"What's the alternative?"

"For sure, a departmental trial," he said. "At least a bust to probationary patrolman and more likely a total boot. Then quite likely a criminal trial, a civil suit, an award against you of several thousand dollars and a ride out of town on a splintery rail. Then there's the dark side of the picture. If you stick around..."

"Spare me the dark side," I said. I took the pen which Lehman had been rhythmically thrusting at me. I know when I'm licked if not much else. But just before starting to sign, I looked up at Lehman and asked, "A private buzzer for sure?"

"For sure," he said. "Sign."

"Leave town for six months—today?"

"Today," Lehman said. "What time do you have?"

"Nearly noon," I said, peeking at the cracked crystal of my Executive Timex.

"Sign that thing and get out of the building within five minutes. Don't worry about your locker. I'll hold your stuff. And be across the city limits by two o'clock at the latest. After that, I can't guarantee you a thing."

"What about sleep?" I asked. "I've been up since the year one. Behind the wheel of a car I'm a menace to the public welfare."

"You'll sleep better out of San Francisco. Believe me."

"My apartment," I said. I really had a very nice apartment.

"Your balls," said Lehman, a bit crudely, I thought.

I know when to give in, and I quickly scrawled my best go-to-hell signature and threw the paper at him.

"You're smarter than I thought you were," said Lehman, grabbing the resignation. He held out a big hand. "Good luck, Joe," he said, "although I'm the one who needs it. You've got five minutes to clear the building." He started toward the half-glass door.

"But, Ralph," I said, "where will I go?" I really wanted to know. He stopped with his hand on the doorknob.

"They say that Mexico is very nice this time of year." The door closed behind him.

"Yeah," I said, too tired to get up, "hot as hell."

3

I walked quickly out of the big, loaf-of-bread police building, expecting at any moment a cry of "Stop that former detective!" The aging traffic lieutenant who gave me a friendly, disinterested nod obviously hadn't yet heard a thing. I'd have made a hell of a good aging traffic lieutenant someday, but I wasn't going to get the chance. I fished my dirty gray Morris convertible from between two Detroit monsters, and joined the midmorning traffic.

It was just a few minutes' drive across Market Street to the small blind alley a couple of blocks off Broadway where I lived. The colorless line of late Victorian houses looked down at me drably. From force of habit I leaned the Morris against a "No Parking" sign and walked into the small grocery store on the street floor.

It was so long since I'd slept that I'd stopped being sleepy. I felt curiously alert and quite detached for a man being run out of town on two hours' notice.

"Lum here?" I asked the latest of a series of boyishly thin Chinese girls to work in the shop.

"Back room," she said, still stuffing small cans of Chinese vegetables into a string bag.

The passage to the back of the shop was so crowded with boxes and crates that I had to crab-walk into the tiny office where Lum Kee, my landlord, sat at a wobbly card table writing in Chinese characters in a big account book. He didn't look up. From the top he looked like a fat and glossy otter just rising from a pool of rubbish. "Lum," I said.

"I know," said Lum, still not looking up from his ledger, "you've shot the mayor's father and you're on the run. It was on the radio this morning. Jon Thatcher's show. You'd better get out of here. I can't afford to harbor a criminal."

Lum Kee stretched an ink-stained, hairless hand out toward the telephone on the card table. I put a hand and about sixty pounds of pressure on the telephone receiver. "Don't be in such a rush to stand by me, Kee," I said. "It gets me all choked up. You're wrong on at least two counts. It wasn't his father, and I'm not on the run. So don't get your hopes up. I haven't got any time to waste, but I'm going out of town for about six months, and—"

"You'll be giving up the apartment?" said Lum Kee brightly. "You'll have to lose your month's deposit, of course, but—"

"No," I said firmly, "I'm not giving up the place. You know that." Five years before, in a time of unexplained panic, Lum Kee had wanted a cop on the premises. He let me have the apartment at a ridiculously low rent and had been regretting it ever since. It had been a false panic, but the apartment was still a great bargain.

"You'll get your rent. But I want you to keep an eye on things, keep the mail for me, that sort of thing. And don't try any fast ones while I'm gone. I'll be back."

I turned and started to leave the tiny room overhung with

cardboard boxes, when Lum Kee said: "Six months' rent is a lot of money to pay for a place you won't even be living in. It seems a shame." His voice conveyed not sympathy for me but sorrow at the pure waste of it all.

"You got a better idea?" I asked, half turning back.

"I have a nephew," he said. "A fine boy. From Honolulu. He's over here taking a course at the San Francisco Bible College. Twenty-six weeks. He might be interested in subletting your place. Pay the same rent and everything, so it wouldn't cost you a thing. I'll write up the contract myself. Just as a favor to you."

"Nephew?" I asked suspiciously.

"My sister Pansy's youngest boy," he said. "He's going to be a missionary. A fine profession."

I didn't care at all for the idea of some Hawaiian religious fanatic using my apartment. But the thought of several hundred dollars flowing from my malnourished bank account into Lum Kee's fat pockets was even more distasteful.

"Where is the Bible banger now?" I asked.

Lum Kee shrugged. "You needn't worry about that. I'll take care of everything. Trust me."

I stiffened my defenses. "I'd rather trust Kolchik," I said. "I'm not subletting to anybody without meeting him first."

"I'll have him up at your apartment in twenty minutes," said Kee, "with the contract."

"That's better," I said, looking at my watch. Twenty minutes of my two hours had already been eaten away. "See that you do." Once again I turned to leave the office. As I got to the passage and turned sideways, I heard Lum Kee say, "The fat one is up at your place waiting."

I kept walking. I knew what he was talking about. But I was thinking of other things as I climbed the three flights of stairs over Lum Kee's shop to my apartment. In my weakened state, the rich cooking odors from the apartment on the first floor made my legs go momentarily wobbly. But when I reached the top of the stairs I was faced with a familiar sight—a small, plump man sitting on the hall carpet with his back to my door. I reached out a hand and helped him to his feet.

"I hope you haven't been waiting too long," I said, opening the door.

"Oh, it hasn't been too bad," he said. "I while away the hours thinking about how much I'm being paid to haunt you." He was plump in a pork-sausage way: sleek, tight, seemingly stretched near the bursting point. He wore a smooth sharkskin suit just a fraction too small in every dimension, and his black hair was not so much thin as uniformly and widely spaced. He was panting slightly from the exertion of getting to his feet.

I pushed past my visitor through the rectangular living room into my long, thin bedroom and began pulling a couple of suitcases from under the bed.

"Do you want to put some coffee on?" I called. "Make lots of it—and strong."

"Okay," he called. After a short silence, I heard the cupboard door creak open and the coffee jar land on the Formica sink. The cold water tap rattled into action.

My apartment wasn't big. It had just one fairly good-sized bedroom and another small room, in theory a bedroom, but actually the graveyard of anything broken or not currently in use. But each of the rooms, even the closet-sized bathroom, offered a mildly spectacular view of San Francisco and the bay, for which a richer person than I would have paid much more rent. That is, if Lum Kee could have gotten me out. I looked down into a half-empty drawer of underwear and socks, wondering which to take. Finally I dumped the whole drawer into my worn canvas suitcase on the bed. Reaching into the big closet I grabbed hangered clothes at random and stuck them into the other case. With a wardrobe like mine, the choice wasn't difficult.

"Coffee's ready."

I came out of the bedroom and found my fat friend sitting on the long couch in front of the bay window, pouring coffee. He handed me a big, brown mug.

"Thanks," I said, letting myself fall to one end of the couch and leaning back with my feet straight out on a cushion. I closed my eyes and took a drink of the hot, bitter coffee.

"I understand you're in a bit of trouble," he said.

"How do you understand that?"

"The late edition of the *Chronicle* and—"

"—the Jon Thatcher Show," I finished for him.

"—and the Thatcher Show. He's making you into a regular feature: The Adventures of Goodey Two-Shoes: Crime Buster."

"Wonderful," I said. "I'm deeply flattered. Have you got the *Chronicle*?"

"Here." He offered me a neatly folded copy of the paper.

"Forget it," I said, pushing the paper away. "I don't think I could take it in my condition."

"Why don't you just give her the divorce, Joe?" he asked with a new, apparently sincere warmth in his voice. "With this latest trouble, you don't need me around your neck. You've got enough problems."

I couldn't help agreeing. For the last three months, the little man—a lawyer's investigator from New York—had been plaguing me to give Pat a divorce. His name was Seymour Kroll, but I had preferred to call him Fatso, Fattie, Lard Ass and finally Chub, as I'd become used to him, and even fond of the little investigator in the way that a hunchback might come to accept the growth between his shoulders. He was better than no company at all.

I wasn't sure myself why I wouldn't give Pat a divorce. She'd been back in New York with her family for almost a year now. I'd long ago packed everything that was hers, including the wedding photographs and an ashtray full of her cigarette butts, and shipped it—collect—to her. That was last winter, right after my flying trip to New York had been such a disaster. After I'd harangued her for days, Pat had gone into hiding. Her father, the very rich Solomon Berkowitz—who for reasons I can't fathom likes to be called Sonny—had seen that I was put on the plane back here by two polite but very determined plain-clothes cops. They didn't want to believe that I, too, was a detective. Once I'd convinced them, they'd been very sympathetic. But they'd still put me on the plane.

"I can't do it, Chub," I told him. "I've got too much on my mind right now to deal with such small matters. It looks as though I'm going to have a lot of time to do some heavy thinking. Maybe I'll come to the conclusion that Pat can have her divorce and marry that jerk." On going back to New York, Pat, who was calling herself Pat Berkowitz again, had taken a job with a big advertising agency. Now it seemed that she wanted to marry some up-and-coming vice president of the agency. The one I'd tried to punch in the mouth last January.

"Where are you going, Joe?"

"I don't know exactly. South. Somebody I know recommends Mexico highly. I'll lie on the beach and get tan."

"That sounds expensive," he said. "How are you going to manage it? You're not exactly flush these days."

"No," I agreed. "How much have I got in the bank, exactly?" Chub peeked into a small black-leather notebook. "$142.76 in the checking and $760.09 in the savings account. That's not very much to go on, and I assume you're not going to have your police salary anymore."

"I've got a week and a half's pay coming," I said.

"Okay, but that's still only a little over a thousand dollars altogether. Look Joe, I'm sure that Mr. Berkowitz would authorize a loan—a substantial loan—if…"

"If is right," I said, finishing my second cup of coffee. "Sonny Berkowitz would be glad to lend me a finger if he was sure of getting an arm back. No deal. No divorce. I'll get along somehow." I wished I could believe that myself. "Look, I've got to get the hell out of here."

"Do you mind if I make a telephone call?" Kroll asked.

"Go ahead," I said. "I'll be packing."

As I walked toward the bedroom, I heard him begin: "Hello, Operator, I want to make a credit-card call to New York City…"

I was barely back in the bedroom when the doorbell gave two raspy bleats. Chub was still murmuring into the mouthpiece when I opened the door and found myself looking at a spot just over the head of a neatly dressed Chinese in his early twenties. The blue wool suit was sincere, and the white shirt front and collar were practically blinding. A black knit tie was transfixed by a tiny gold crucifix. His smooth, oval face was pleasant, even if the mouth hinted of primness.

"You're the nephew."

"That's right, Mr. Goodey," he said, holding out a short-fingered hand. "My name is Gabriel Fong. May I come in?"

I gave him what I hoped passed for a welcoming handshake and stepped backward into the living room.

"Sure. Have a look around."

I had a look around myself and suddenly realized just how bare and anonymous the place was without Pat's things. It could have been a rather shabby hotel room.

Just then Kroll stopped talking and put his hand over the receiver. "Joe," he said, "could you spare a moment? Mr. Berkowitz would like to speak to you."

"No," I said, feeling surly, "I've got to get packed and out of the city"—I looked at my watch—"in less than an hour. Tell Sonny I'll write him a letter—with a bomb in it."

Kroll held the receiver up in front of him in an imploring gesture. His small, close-set eyes begged me to be reasonable, be kind, be human.

"All right," I said, "what the hell." Walking toward the telephone, I told the nephew, "Have a good look around. I won't be long." Taking the receiver, slightly damp, slightly warm, I put on my most bored voice, and it didn't take much acting.

"Hello Sonny. Did you hear the good news?"

"Now, Joe," said his Lower Second Avenue voice overlaid with Harvard and thirty years of good living, "you know better than that. I wish you no ill. I've got nothing against you. I only want Patricia to be happy, and the only thing I know that can make her happy is for you to give her a divorce. Joe, you must understand. Pat's in love. She wants to marry Ernest."

"I'm touched," I said, "deeply touched. But the answer's the same. If Pat wants a divorce, she'll either have to come back here or wait out the divorce laws there. I'm not going to make it any easier. Now, if you'll excuse me, I haven't been to sleep for so long that I forget what it's like, and I've got some fast moving to do. Goodbye, Sonny, give—"

"Joe," said my practically ex-father-in-law in a voice so sincere that I felt like the rat I really was, "Seymour said there was no point in mentioning it, but I know that with no paycheck coming in things are going to be a bit tight for you. Listen, with no strings attached, I could let you have a small loan, hell, a medium loan, just to keep you going until you connect with something else. No strings, Joe, no strings at all."

"I believe it, Sonny," I told him, "but no thanks. I'm loaded with money, no matter what Seymour tells you. Now, I've got to go. I'm giving you back to Seymour." I handed the still-talking receiver to a sorrowful Seymour and turned my attention to the Bible student, who was standing at the bay window looking out past Coit Tower at the Richmond-San Rafael Bridge sticking out of the haze. I joined him.

"What do you think?"

"It looks just fine to me, Mr. Goodey," he said. "Here's the contract my uncle drew up. I hope everything is satisfactory."

He handed me a long sheet of accounting paper half covered with tiny writing. I skimmed it quickly. I knew that if Lum Kee wanted to hide some joker clauses I'd never find them anyway. It all seemed fairly straightforward.

"It looks okay," I said, "but I don't really like the idea of leaving my apartment to anybody." I peered closely at Fong, bringing out my I'm-a-keen-copper-so-don't-try-to-bullshit-me look. "I only hope you're nowhere near as big a crook as Lum Kee. I couldn't stand it."

"I'm not," he said, apparently neither knocked over by my look nor offended. "One of the things my mother asked me to do while I am here is to try to put my uncle's feet back on the path of righteousness."

"You've got a big job," I told him. "I don't think Lum's feet were ever within taxi distance of it. But I'm wasting time. The place is yours for six months—no more. If you or your uncle double-cross me, I'll come back and get you both. I'm a hard man. Ask Mayor Kolchik." Having failed to impress Fong, I turned to Chub, who was just hanging up the telephone.

"Chub, come here and witness this legal document."

We all three signed the contract, and Fong left, agreeing to pick up the key to my apartment at his uncle's store. I jumped back into the bedroom and locked my packed cases. Bringing them out into the living room, I put the cases down by the door and turned to Seymour. "Well, Chub—" I held out my hand.

His jaw dropped. On that round face the fall couldn't have been fatal.

"You're not going to try to lose me, are you, Joe," he asked. "Mr. Berkowitz's instructions are to stick with you wherever you go. It's my job. Besides, he's authorized me to lend you any reasonable amount if you need it. That might come in handy, Joe. Think about it."

I thought for five seconds. "All right, but I'm not waiting for you a single minute. Your hotel is not far from my bank. I've got to draw some money, and if you're there in exactly thirty minutes, you can come with me. It'll save Sonny the cost of renting a car."

"You promise, Joe?"

"I promise." I tried to look sincere and probably succeeded only in looking sinister.

"All right then," he said still a bit doubtfully, "I'll get going. I'll meet you on the corner of Market and Montgomery, right in front of the Bank of America."

"Okay, Chub, but don't be late or you'll get left. I'm supposed to be out of this town by two o'clock."

Kroll left wearing an expression torn between hopeful trust and wistful misgiving, and I took a last look around.

Feeling like a vagrant, I picked up my bags, went out into the hall, kicking the door shut behind me, and started down the steep stairs. On the street I threw the cases into the back of the Morris— triumphantly unticketed—and walked into Lum Kee's.

"He's out," said the skinny girl behind the counter coldly.

"I don't care," I said to show that I didn't. I separated the door key from my malnourished key ring and dropped it into the girl's uneager hand.

"Give this extremely valuable key to Lum Kee," I said, "and

tell him that if he crosses me I'll cut his heart out and make him eat it."

This didn't get a rise out of her either, but she took the key.

I climbed into the battered convertible and made an illegal turn. In less than a minute, I was on Broadway heading west, almost directly away from the corner of Market and Montgomery.

"Sorry, Chub, old buddy," I murmured hypocritically as the car entered the Broadway tunnel.

4

THE HOUSES FLANKING BROADWAY WERE PALE, COOL, AND slightly aloof, with just enough patchy color to ward off anonymity. At Van Ness Avenue I snaked across onto Lombard as if I were going to head north on Route 101 into Marin County. That's what we police call misleading and evasive tactics. After a few blocks I pulled into a Shell station.

"Fill it up and check everything," I told a teenaged desperado who slunk out to the pumps, jamming a rolled-up underground newspaper into his hip pocket. At a telephone booth near the sidewalk, I put a dime in the slot and dialed a number in Sausalito. Three rings later, a high-pitched voice said, "Hello?"

"Hello, Ramsey," I said. "This is Joe. Let me speak to your mother."

"Hi, Joe, when are you coming to see us?"

"Soon," I lied, looking at my watch. It was twenty after one. "Is your mother there?"

"Gee, Joe—" I could hear a slight scuffle on the other end of the line, and Rachel Schute's husky voice came on. "Hello, Joe," she said. "It's been a long time."

"Yes," I said flatly, unwilling to start meaningless explanations. "Look, Rachel, I haven't got much time. I called mostly to say that a bit of a situation has come up, and I've got to go away for a while. Last night—"

"I heard," she said. "How's the old man?"

"Okay, I think. Last report from the hospital said he wasn't particularly cheerful but would pull through. I'm not so sure Cousin Sanford will. How did you hear? The Chronicle? Thatcher?"

"Neither. People have been calling all day."

"Yeah, and I can imagine who they were, too. But I haven't much time. I'm just on my way out of town."

"I thought you'd be just on your way to jail if I know Kolchik at all." She sounded really concerned. And I felt even more guilty.

"Naw," I said, "Lehman claims he can work a deal for me. I handed in my badge and agreed to disappear for six months while Kolchik cools off and gets himself re-elected."

"Six months is a long time, Joe," she said in that grave, even voice I knew so well. "Where do you plan to go?"

"No plans at all," I admitted. "But Mexico looks like a strong contender."

"Why Mexico?"

"Why not Mexico?"

"Are you going alone?" There was no complaint, no plea in her voice, but the words were heavy with what I knew they left unsaid.

"Yes," I said shortly. How do you stretch out a one-word answer? But I added: "As soon as I know where I'm going to be, I'll let you know. I'll send you an address."

"You do that, Joe," she said. "I'll be glad to hear. We all will. Thanks for calling. But, Joe, one thing—"

"Yeah?" I said wearily, expecting the worst.

"Don't try to go too far today. You sound like you're going to sleep on your feet. You're tripping over your words."

"You're right," I said, feeling the fuzziness heavy upon me again. "I won't. Take care, Rachel, and give my love to the boys."

"I will," she said and hung up the telephone.

The pump jockey was waiting impatiently. Two cars were lined up behind the Morris.

"That'll be a buck ninety-five," he said, holding out a small hand.

"Did you check the battery water?"

"I forgot," said the attendant. "That'll be a buck ninety-five."

"Do it now," I said, wondering why I was wasting valuable time.

"Look—" the boy said, turning his eyes toward the line-up of customers.

"The line will only get longer," I said like a kindly uncle.

Mouthing a nice, if limited, line of curses, the boy threw himself toward the station office, came lurching back with the distilled water bottle, and wrenched up the hood of my Morris. His enraged fingers twisted off the battery caps and spilled half the water on the concrete. He put the caps on, slammed the hood down, and turned back to me.

"That okay?" he said savagely.

"Just fine," I said approvingly, handing him two dollars.

The boy didn't even see the money. He was concentrating on me, willing me to disappear.

"My change," I said. "Five cents. Or make it a nickel."

The attendant clawed into his tight pocket and came up with a handful of keys and small change which he thrust toward my face like a knockout punch. I looked it over, took a nickel and climbed back into my car. You're a bastard, Goodey, I told myself.

Continuing west on Lombard, I ignored the turn north to the Golden Gate Bridge and went on through the Presidio, heading for the beach and the road south. I was thinking about Rachel Schute.

She was the closest thing I'd had to a steady woman since Pat had left. But not that steady. Rachel was a remarkable woman—pretty in a delicate-skinned, red-haired, high-strung way, intelligent, affectionate, and easy to be with. Her three boys liked me as much as she obviously did. For me, Rachel had only two drawbacks, but they were big ones. She was forty-four years old and a millionairess several times over. Not that I have anything against money. Though there's something about rich women—even Rachel—that makes me nervous. But the biggest problem for me was her age. I couldn't see any way around that. I'm the kind of stupid jerk who likes them young and firm—like Pat—and moldable. In a slightly drunken moment Rachel had once said that real women scared me. Maybe she was right.

Soon I was rounding Sutro Heights and heading down the familiar road running along Ocean Beach. On the left, Playland lay sprawled like a gypsy camp. The orange and yellow canvas had a desolate gaiety. The sea was calm, with just a scattering of whitecaps. I'd walked this beat for over a year when I was a rookie. I could still feel the biting cold and hear the ragged music from the old merry-go-round at Playland.

Continuing south, hugging the coastline, I pushed the old Morris past Lake Merced until I came to the familiar San Francisco City Limits sign. I looked at my watch. It was ten of two.

Ten minutes' grace. I had made it. But I felt fatigue hit me like a sandbag behind the left ear. My eyes closed involuntarily, and it seemed to take ages to wrench one of them open and stay on the road. I knew I had to sleep.

A little farther along I caught a sign on the right side of the road: Seavue Lodge—Vacancy. Driving over a grass-cracked sidewalk, I pulled the car up slightly askew against a white-washed timber railing and let the engine die of its own accord. With great effort, I reached up and switched off the ignition, but my hand fell back before I could pinch enough to remove the key. Moving as I imagine zombies—tired zombies—do, I eased myself out of the car and pushed toward a screen door at the front of a big old house with a pink stucco addition tacked on at the side.

"A room," I said to a pleasant-faced old body with gray hair sitting behind a short desk, knitting something orange. I could read her mind as she sniffed at me and then decided I wasn't drunk. She opened a faded black registration book on the desk.

"Is seven dollars okay?" she asked.

"Fine," I said with effort. I scrawled something in the book and held out my hand. "The key."

She reached up to a peg board behind her, took down a large brass key with a wooden tag marked "8," and handed it to me. I nearly dropped it.

"Luggage?" she said.

"In the car," I managed to squeeze out. "Later." I stood in front of the counter, knowing that there was something I wanted to ask but unable to think what it was.

"Through that side door," the woman said, pointing, "and turn right. It's the third door on the left."

I cleverly followed her instructions and found myself facing a door carrying the number "8" painted in shiny black. With profound relief I saw that the door was open a crack and pushed through it. I scarcely saw a big, sagging iron bed covered with what looked like cotton candy before I hit it with all my weight.

5

It was broad, broad daylight again when I woke up with a faceful of fuzzy bed cover. I rolled over on my back on the swaybacked bed and saw Ralph Lehman sitting in a chair in front of the window, looking at me with the eyes of a 225-pound Jesus Christ. One of his big feet was resting on one of my suitcases.

I closed my eyes again, hoping that he'd go away. But he remained—fat, tired, getting old, but still there. A glance down told me I was still fully clothed, but some kind soul had removed my shoes. I knew I'd been asleep for a long time because I felt queerly rested and very hungry.

"What day is it?" I asked, once I could get a little saliva flowing again. Someone had been blotting up mud with my tongue. "Friday," Ralph said. "One o'clock. Joe—"

"Don't Joe me, you son of a bitch."

"Joe," he said.

"You lying bastard. You promised. Just leave town, Joe, you said, give up a brilliant police career and disappear, and everything will be all right. I'll fix it. I'll dazzle Sanford and The

Brother with my faultless footwork, and there'll be no sweat. That's what you said. You, Chief of Detectives Ralph C. Lehman, said that. Tired as I was, I heard you. And now this, you prick."

"Joe," he said, "are you finished?"

"No, but I'm taking a breather. What do you have to say?"

"You promise you'll listen? Really listen?"

"I'll listen, but I don't promise to like it."

"You'll like it," he said. "Joe, I meant every word I said yesterday morning. And things went very smoothly. The mayor and his high-ranking brother weren't very happy about your escaping alive, but I sweet-talked them. I told them how it was. And they bought it, Joe. They bought it."

"So what are you doing here?"

"You said you'd listen. Now, shut up."

"I'm shut up."

"Okay. That was yesterday. But things have changed since then, Joe."

I opened my mouth again, but Ralph pointed a thick finger toward it, so I shut up.

"Things have changed," he said, "because at about three o'clock this morning Tina D'Oro was found murdered in her apartment over The Jungle."

I didn't have to hide astonishment, because I didn't feel any. Or any emotion other than a vague feeling you might get when you heard that a public landmark you didn't feel much for had been pulled down. More of a feeling that I should feel something.

"And you think I did it, Ralph? You're more senile than the boys in the squad room think. If you—"

"No, no, no," Ralph said with the consummate weariness of a man whose last year before retirement looks as if it's going to last forever. "I don't think you did it. Now, just listen, for Christ's sake." He looked at his watch. "We haven't got much time. Bruno Kolchik expects us in his office by three o'clock."

I let that pass. "Go on," I said, sitting down on the bed.

"When Tina was found, she had been dead for close to twenty-four hours. At that time, we know where you were. You were busy shooting the mayor's cousin. That's a damned fine alibi. But it's also beside the point. In plain, simple language Tina D'Oro's diary was found in her apartment, and featured prominently in that diary was the name of a man we all know and love."

"Ralph Lehman," I said, just for the hell of it.

"Sanford F. Kolchik," Ralph said.

Then I was surprised, and I didn't try to hide it. "Sandy Kolchik, our revered mayor and maybe prospective governor, messing around with the queen of the go-go girls? You're kidding. Even Sanford's not that stupid."

"I'm not. And he is. But fortunately, a young detective with a brilliant police career ahead of him stumbled on the diary and stashed it before the press arrived."

"Which is a contravention of every law I can think of and could get that brilliant detective, you and Sanford many years if it comes out."

"If it comes out," Lehman agreed. "But in the meantime it's got Johnny Maher promoted to detective sergeant, and—"

"Not the Johnny Maher who's such an opportunistic and sucking-up little bastard?"

"The very same," Lehman said. "But, more important, it gives you a little time, a very little time, to find out who killed Tina."

"Me? Why do I want to do that?"

"Well, partly, as you may have heard, because Kolchik would sort of like to be re-elected."

I laughed, not a very nice laugh. "I wish him a whole lot of luck."

"He's wishing you the same. Because his future is very much tied in with yours. If you don't come back to San Francisco and find out who killed Tina, he's going to do all those things I promised you he'd do. Remember?"

"I remember," I said, and I did. All too well. "But why me, Ralph? Yesterday morning Kolchik didn't seem to think I had much promise as a detective...as I remember."

"He still doesn't. He thinks you're a fuck-up. But you've got two things going for you. You're off the force, so you can operate in a private capacity. And you knew Tina. That makes you the man for the job."

He was right on both counts. I certainly was off the police, and I knew Tina, if only casually. A couple of years before, I'd had to fill in for a couple of weeks on the North Beach squad, and somebody was shot to death at The Jungle, the nightclub she was supposed to own a hunk of. While I was brushing away the flies and waiting for the homicide bunch to take over, Tina came over and sat on a bar stool near me. She was in costume—that is, she had almost nothing on—but she'd thrown an old chenille bathrobe over her shoulders. She was sitting at the bar, sipping on a tall drink and peering at a paperback book through thick, horn-rimmed glasses that definitely were not part of her act. She looked up with a puzzled expression and, since no one else was very close, asked me a question.

"Which is the one where you throw up," she wanted to know, "resuscitation or regurgitation?"

I took a wild guess and told her the second one. The book turned out to be Thirty Days to a Vocabulary Like a High-School Graduate, and we started talking about long and funny words—a highbrow conversation which was soon broken up by the murder boys, and I disappeared.

But sometime later, after I'd gone back to the commercial squad, I was eating alone one night at Fettucini's, and somebody sat down at the table with me. Tina. "How's your vocabulary?" I said for lack of anything more intelligent, and we talked for a while. After that, every so many weeks I'd run into her, and we'd talk. Me about the trouble I was having with Pat. Her about her search for an improved word power. Both sad stories.

It wasn't what you'd call a long and close relationship. But behind those spectacular tits and the brassy blond hair and the flat, dumb little face, there seemed to be a person. Not the brightest, maybe too ambitious, but a person who had nothing much to do with swinging boobs and loud music.

"All right, Ralph," I said, "I'll give you that. I knew Tina—slightly. But that doesn't mean I can tell you who killed her. Are you sure Kolchik didn't do it?"

"He says he didn't," Lehman said, "and I sort of give him the benefit of the doubt. But I'm not worried. You'll find out who did it, and you'll find out pretty soon. Without the sacred name of Kolchik coming into the case."

"Or what?" I asked, knowing the answer.

"Joe, I don't have to tell you that. Don't make me go through it again. I feel crappy enough doing Sanford's dirty work as it is. Can't you look on this as an opportunity, Joe? It gets you out from behind the eight ball. It gets you back on the payroll. The mayor's apparently got a little fund for such delicate matters. Every week, your old salary will go into your bank account."

"And expenses, Ralph," I said. "Those lousy private operatives always get expenses. Don't forget that."

"And expenses," Lehman said, looking more cheerful. "Thank God you're beginning to make sense. Look on the bright side, Joe. You get your private buzzer right away, and if all goes well, you get a good shot at getting back your old job."

"You're a real sport, Ralph," I said, but I knew I had no other real choice.

"Let's get cracking," he said. "We're going to have to move if we're going to make that appointment with Bruno."

I showered vigorously, brushed my teeth, shaved, dressed again, and followed Lehman out of the room. He carried my suitcases just as he'd brought them in from my car.

The woman with the orange knitting was behind the desk again, and she looked at me as if I were Public Enemy Number One. She glanced down at my wrists, and I knew she was looking for handcuffs.

I didn't want to disappoint her entirely, so I scowled and jerked a thumb at Lehman. "This guy will pay the bill," I said. I pushed through the screen door into the soft, midday sunshine. Lehman's big Mercury stood next to my small convertible, and a young patrolman leaned on it and looked at me with curious eyes.

"Get in with me, Goodey," Ralph said, coming out of the motel office. "This nice young man will be happy to drive your wreck into town for you." The rookie scuttled out of our way toward the Morris, and I flipped him the keys.

"He'd better be a careful driver," I said as I settled into the Mercury's big, soft seats, "or the mayor will be buying me another car."

"Find out who murdered Tina," Ralph said, starting the engine, "without splashing shit on Kolchik, and he'll buy you a new Cadillac."

6

LEHMAN RELUCTANTLY STOPPED AT A ROADSIDE restaurant and balefully stared at me while I ripped through a city-paid-for steak. The city got robbed, but I felt like a better man. As we got back into Ralph's Mercury, I looked longingly at the highway south. Mexico was going to have to wait.

Our second stop was the coroner's meat room down in the bottom of the Hall of Justice. It felt funny to be walking into a building I thought I'd said goodbye to just yesterday. It hadn't changed a lot. We went down a set of outside steps at the back, because I wasn't supposed to be there.

Smokey Sefton, the assistant ghoul, pulled out what looked like a filing cabinet drawer, flipped back a rubber blanket, and there was Tina, lying on her back with those fantastic tits sticking up like howitzer shells. Her skin was the color of old, weatherworn marble, gray-white, and with a vague coarseness. The famous body was unmarked except for a nasty appendix scar and a rather triangular wound just above and slightly to the right of her left breast, made by the blade that had nicked an artery and spilled her life's blood. The interns had done a good job of cleaning her up, but they didn't know much about the latest hair styles.

"Fucking amazing," said Ralph, exaggeratedly bug-eyeing Tina's body. "Bet you've been having a good time for yourself down here, eh, Smokey? I'd hate to have that body dusted for prints. Put you away for life."

Smokey, a little man with the mouth of a deacon's wife, gave him a shadow of a smile. "You through with her?" he asked.

"Not really," said Lehman. "I was going to ask if I could take her home for the weekend. I promise to have her back first thing Monday morning."

"Yeah," I said, "put her away." I'd seen enough. Tina hadn't changed much below the neck, but above she was nearly unrecognizable. The mask of make-up and animation had been ripped away, leaving a face that was a little hard, a little dumb, a little vacant—nothing you'd pay two fifty a drink to see. They say some stiffs look like they're sleeping. Tina's face looked like she was waiting for a very late bus on a cold, wet night, and her feet hurt. They should have put her on the stage of The Jungle just like that. It would have set the topless go-go business back a century.

"Come on," I told Lehman, "you can sneak back later after Smokey goes home. I suppose all the paperwork is upstairs?"

"Yeah," said Lehman when we'd left Sefton and Tina behind and gotten into the thin, green-doored elevator that would take us to the top of the building—once again the discreet, back-door way. "Everything is in The Brother's office. He wants to see you."

"I can't say the same. But what about Smokey? Isn't he going to think it's peculiar that I resigned yesterday and came down to cop a peek at Tina today?"

"Smokey can't afford to think anything's peculiar," Ralph

said. "He likes his job. Besides, he's been down in the morgue so long I think he's lost contact with reality."

"Lucky him."

The elevator banged to a stop, and we stepped out, across a wide hall and through a door marked "Bruno D. Kolchik, Deputy Chief." His secretary, a skinny blonde with an I-dare-you-to-kiss-me mouth and dangling jade earrings, looked up from the novel she was reading.

"Oh, hello," she said graciously, marking her place with a long finger. "The chief has been expecting you, but he's out for a few moments. If you'll take a seat..." She waved her free hand toward a pair of forbidding courtroom chairs against the wall.

Feeling nasty, I looked even more blank than usual. "The chief?" I said. "But we're here to see Bruno Kolchik, formerly Sergeant Kolchik of the Parks Division—you know, a big, beefy guy with hairy red ears and a face like a broken knee. If we've come to the wrong office..."

"Shut up, Joe," said Lehman.

She was working her mouth like a poisoned pike, but nothing was coming out. Just as she was about to start pinching herself to see if she was having a nightmare, her boss shouldered the door aside like a tent flap and nearly trampled us. Except that people the size of Ralph Lehman don't get trampled. People my size do. The Brother didn't look happy.

"I've been expecting you," he said to Lehman. He didn't even look at me, but charged through the space I'd been occupying and disappeared into his office. I assumed we were supposed to follow. Lehman did, but I lingered to have a word with the blonde.

"Remember," I said, "snitchers never prosper. Besides, he might be a sergeant again someday." But she'd forgotten I existed and was trying to find her place in her book.

"What the hell kept you?" Bruno yelled at me when I came

through the door into his big office. He had a cut-glass decanter in one hand and a tall glassful of ice cubes in the other. Lehman had settled into the most comfortable chair in the room and was staring patiently out the vast windows.

"She wouldn't let me go without a goodbye kiss," I said. "You know how some broads are."

He didn't like that, and his ears deepened three shades of red. One thing about The Brother: he not only had the title of Deputy Chief, he thought he was Deputy Chief. Some guys who'd been a sergeant for fifteen years until their brother was elected mayor and then suddenly found themselves number two man of the whole force would be sheepish about it. Not Bruno. The way he acted, you'd think he'd passed a civil service test for the job. The trouble was that he'd have made a swell lost-property clerk, and that's probably what he'd be if and when his brother wasn't mayor anymore. So long to the three stars on the shoulder and the cut-glass decanter.

"Watch it, Goodey," he said, pointing the decanter at me as if he wished it were a gun. He splashed a little Scotch on the Persian carpet. "I don't like you, and you're only out of the clink as long as you make yourself useful and watch your smart mouth."

"I don't like you, either," I said, reaching out and taking the decanter. There was no glass at hand, so I took a polite swig from the decanter. "And you're only in this office as long as your brother is mayor. That won't be long if it gets out that he killed Tina D'Oro." Even The Brother wasn't too dense to realize that what I said was true. So, instead of exploding, he took a long, ice-cube-tinkling gulp of his drink and came out of the experience a much calmer man.

"But the mayor didn't kill her," he said. "We know that. Your job is to find out who did. And to do it fast. We're sitting on a time bomb, and if it goes off before the killer is safely behind bars, we're all going down with the ship." His direct gaze took in Lehman as well as me. "And I mean all."

"What I want to know," I said, "is why you think you need me. You've got a fistful of aces here. Why the hell do you want a busted detective cluttering things up? Let homicide earn its money."

"Don't think they won't," he said. "Maher is handling that end of the operation. And he's got the word that he can go down as fast as he came up. He'll be doing his best. But the mayor thought it might be useful to have someone else on the job. Someone with maybe more flexibility than the homicide crew and a personal interest in finding the killer."

"Like his own survival?" I asked.

His eyes nodded, if eyes can do that sort of thing.

"And maybe somebody who'd be tempted to bend the law just a little bit in the interest of the same. Somebody ripe for a fall if things get too sticky," I added.

This time his eyes shrugged. "You do anything illegal," he said, "you do it on your own hook. As far as the world knows, you're just an ex-copper out to make a living behind a private buzzer. If you want to look into who spiked Tina D'Oro, nobody can tell you no."

"Speaking of that buzzer," I said, "I assume you've got it for me."

Bruno walked over behind his big desk and picked up a thin file folder. "It's in here," he said, holding the folder out toward me, "along with the coroner's report on Tina and a copy of Maher's report from the scene of the crime. Take it."

I let him hold it for a while. He had strong arms.

"And Tina's diary?" I asked.

"The diary has been destroyed," he said too quickly. "It doesn't exist anymore."

"That's too bad," I said, still not taking the folder, "because if that diary doesn't exist, neither do I." I stuck out both wrists. "Put the cuffs on me, Ralph. I'm ready to stand the rap for Cousin Stanislaus. I'd rather do that than go after Tina's killer blindfolded with both hands tied behind my back. Besides, maybe I'll cop a self-defense plea."

The Brother looked disgustedly at me, then at Lehman. He threw the folder down on his desk and whirled to look out the window at traffic on the Oakland Bay Bridge.

"Joe," said Ralph, "be reasonable. You're talking about a document which, if it still exists, is deeply embarrassing to the mayor and his family. You can't expect—"

"I do expect, Ralph," I said. "And I'm doing nothing without a look at that diary. I don't expect you to give it to me to take home, but I've got to have a good, hard look at it, or I don't budge. Either give me the diary or take me down to the cells."

Lehman didn't say anything, but The Brother turned around and without looking at me walked over to a big Red Period Picasso print and lifted it down from the wall. He twiddled around with a combination knob and opened a round metal door. Fishing out a small book with a red plastic cover, he threw it down on his desk with a loud slap.

"All right," he said to Lehman, "let him look at it. Here. He can take notes, but the diary doesn't leave this office. You understand?" He tried to drill holes in Lehman with his eyes. That's been tried before, and Ralph silently returned the favor. The Brother wheeled and headed for the door.

"Thanks, Bro," I said to his disappearing back.

I picked up the thin diary, sat down in Bruno's big leather chair and put my feet on his desk blotter. Ralph wearily went back to memorizing the area south of Market Street.

Tina D'Oro was no Samuel Pepys. You could pick up more gossip on a bus ticket. If you went by her diary, life as a topless go-go dancer was about as exciting as learning to spotweld. And she didn't even keep it every day. January 1 started out with one big resolution: "I will learn ten new words every week." Nothing more lofty or aspiring than that. The handwriting was junior high school gothic with the cute touch of making the dots over the *i*'s into circles.

Tina tended to keep her diary mostly as a reminder of appointments rather than as a repository of deep, dark secrets. The name that appeared most often was someone called Irma. "Lunch with Irma." "Irma's for a hairdo." "Meet Irma at four." I'd have to meet this Irma. But the most intriguing thing was a series of initials: O.G., F.I. ("Check up with F.I.," the diary said), H.C., J.M.

But then, on March 5, Tina began to throw discretion out the window. "Dinner with the mayor," the diary said. That old dog. Thereafter a certain Mr. Kolchik began to get a lot of space. She spelled his name three different ways, but the inference was clear. Mr. K. was riding high, if that's not too bald for you. Then it became Sandy...Sandy this and Sandy that. Poor Kolchik. If he'd been less important, he'd have been a mere S.K., and the diary could have been found—for the record. The last entry was ten days before: "Movie with Irma."

I took a few notes, but, to tell the truth, Tina's diary wasn't a gold mine for clues. I mean, I had no immediate need for an arrest warrant. Maybe if I'd studied the diary for twenty years I'd have discovered that Tina was really a Russian spy using an elaborate code.

I didn't have twenty years. I flipped through the diary one last time and threw it over to Ralph Lehman.

"There you are, Ralph," I said. "Stick it back in The Brother's safe or eat it, for all I care. I'll have the villain in the pokey by a week Tuesday, or my name's not Sherlock Holmes."

"Your name's not Sherlock Holmes," said Ralph, looking depressed. "You're not even a very good detective."

"Thanks, old truthteller," I said. "I'll see you around." I slouched toward the door, pretending that I was a man who had someplace to go.

"Tell me something, Joe," said Lehman as I put my hand on the doorknob. I looked around at him. "Do you think I'm a terrible shit for going along with the brothers K. this way?" He looked as if he really wanted to know.

So I told him. "Yeah, Ralph, I think you're a terrible shit. But don't look hurt. We're all terrible shits in this business, and you ought to be happy that next year you won't have to be one anymore."

"Thanks," he said, pushing the word out as if it were a two-ton boulder on his chest.

"I suppose you're my contact," I said, "and you'll be hearing from me. But now you tell me something, Ralph. Do you think I'm going to find out who killed Tina?"

He shook his big head. "Not a chance, Joe," he said. "Not a chance in the world."

"I'll try to live up to your faith in me," I said and walked out through Bruno's door. The skinny blonde wasn't there; neither was The Brother. They must have been off someplace holding each other's hands and worrying about the fact that sergeants don't have secretaries. Neither do convicts.

I went out of the police building as I'd come in—the back way. I never liked back doors. They rob you of that comfortable feeling of belonging. Now that feeling was long gone, and with only a thin folder of papers under my arm I felt naked and alone. I'd even have been glad to see Chub just then, but God knows where he was.

The young cop had left my car in the parking lot, but I cut through a tall, thin alley toward Sam's Cafe. Then I remembered that Sam's was a cop hangout, and I was no longer a cop. I took a random right and after about a block was in front of something called Ricardo's Place. The windows looked as if they'd been used for the bottom of a racing pigeon cage.

There was nobody behind the bar. That didn't bother me, and I slipped into a booth in front of the least-dirty window and slid the contents of the file folder out on the slightly sticky table. I was admiring the private operative's license when a voice came out over the bar like a rusty laser beam. "The public library is three blocks over, mate."

"Thanks," I said, looking up at a knobbly, bald Scandinavian head stuck to a long, thin body in a worn-out T-shirt. Tattoos which were vivid on the arms blurred as they disappeared into the T-shirt "If you're Ricardo, you can bring me a double Margarita, easy on the salt."

"We've got only three drinks in this joint," the man said. "Whiskey, whiskey, and beer. In that order."

"That suits me," I said. "In that order. Do you have table service, or is the waitress on strike?"

He brought me a double whiskey and a beer chaser. I paid him, and he did a disappearing trick into the shadows near the bar.

Tucking away my ticket to romance, adventure and poverty, I turned to two of the last documents which would concern themselves with Tina D'Oro. The autopsy report was straightforward in the extreme. The subject had expired due to an excessive loss of blood, which in turn was caused by an undisclosed pointed but not-very-sharp instrument. She'd been dead about twenty-four hours when she was found. She was likely to be dead for a long time. The autopsy report didn't actually say that, but I like to interpret whenever I can.

Johnny Maher's report was a little more convoluted. Leaving out the professional jargon that passes for erudition in the police force, Maher's version was that Tina hadn't turned up for her gig on Thursday night. This was greeted with a certain amount of dismay, the culture lovers being lined up three deep in front of the bar. Somehow a substitute was found to take Tina's place in the show if not in the hearts of the suckers.

Meanwhile, somebody went upstairs and did the doorknob-shaking routine at Tina's apartment. But no answer. The matter was dropped until after the last tourist had been pried from the bar, and The Jungle slammed its doors. Then somebody named Miss Irma Springler—that must be my Irma, I thought—came in looking for Tina. Seems they had a date of some kind. The club manager, Mr. Sherman Bums, told her that Tina hadn't come in for work that evening. Hadn't been seen at all that day, in fact.

Miss Springler got a bit upset. So much so that she went upstairs and started belting Tina's door. Still no answer. Then Miss Springler insisted that somebody find a key for Tina's door and open it. She had a premonition, she said, that something terrible had happened to Tina. A key was found, the door was opened, and there was Tina, still in what was supposed to be a costume, lying in the middle of her living room on an expensive orange rug which had soaked up a whole lot of blood.

The coppers were called, who tugged on Johnny Maher's chain. In his professional opinion there'd been little struggle. Whoever had done it had been known to the victim and hadn't been in her apartment long. Clues to date: none.

This was not exactly the kind of detection likely to get a man promoted, but then Johnny didn't mention the little red diary he'd found, flicked through, and pocketed. Johnny may not have been the best detective in the world, but he had an eye for the main chance. And he'd be going all out to make sure he wound this one up the right way. With His Honor nowhere in sight. There were higher rungs on Maher's ladder than sergeant.

I closed the file, tipped back the rest of the whiskey, and washed it down with the beer. When I left, Ricardo didn't come out to say goodbye, but that was okay by me. I can't take sentimental scenes, and my suit couldn't stand any tear stains. We both knew what we meant to each other.

Walking back to the police parking lot, I decided to go home. Then I remembered that I didn't have a home. I decided to go there anyway. Pulling my car out of the lot, I headed for North Beach.

7

Retrieving the extra key from a crack under a ledge on the front porch, I climbed the stairs to my front door and opened it. Somehow it never occurred to me to knock. The living room was empty. I figured that the Bible banger was out saving souls, and I was heading for the bathroom when something in the bedroom caught my eye. Not to sound too much like one of the three bears, but someone was sleeping in my bed. And it wasn't Goldilocks.

But it was a girl. Automatically tiptoeing, I moved through the bedroom doorway and stood looking down at the sleeper. She was Chinese, with skin like polished silk. A shiny black rope of hair lay coiled over her left shoulder. In my big bed she looked about nine years old, but her face was infinitely older and worn. She had black pouches like bruises under her eyes, and the skin over the minuscule bridge of her turtle nose was drawn so tight it was the non-color of old ivory. One arm like a not particularly sturdy stick of rigatoni lay palm up on top of the covers. An ugly blue-black swollen vein in the crook of her arm told me something about the way she got her kicks. It was like seeing a two-year-old kid with a fifth of gin.

Just as I was waxing moralistic and wondering what the hell my subtenant was up to, something small but compact attached itself to my back, and a pair of hard little hands began trying to put a crimp in my windpipe. I'm easygoing and slow to anger, but this was getting annoying. So I put an elbow where it would do the most good and heard a rewarding "oomph" from the jockey on my back. The hands let loose, and my friend hit the floor behind me with a crash. I turned around and was about to step on the face of a midget in a flashy silk jacket when Gabriel Fong came through the door with both arms full of groceries and an alarmed expression on his face.

"Mickey!" he shouted. This wasn't me, so it must have been the kid crab-walking backward to get out from under my foot. It seemed impolite to stomp him in front of company, so I backed off and let Mickey get to his feet. He wasn't a midget after all, just a Chinese kid of maybe sixteen. The jacket indicated that he belonged to some sort of gang.

Fong found a place to unload the groceries and came back from the kitchen. But it wasn't the same Fong I'd met yesterday. The woolly blue suit and knitted tie were gone. In their place was a pair of beautifully faded Levis, a matching jacket and a bright yellow T-shirt.

Even his hair was different. The missionary cut had been replaced by something spiky and random, as if he'd combed his hair with a Turkish towel. He was still too clean-cut to look scruffy, but he looked like a Bible student's version of hip, and you had to give him credit for trying. The only sign of his calling was a small silver cross dangling on a chain outside his T-shirt.

Fong opened his mouth to say something, but the kid beat

him to it: "He broke in, Gabe," Mickey said. "He was after Fsui-tang. I had to jump him. He—"

"It's okay, Mickey," Fong said soothingly. "This is Mr. Goodey. He's a friend of mine. In fact, this is his apartment. Why don't you go in and sit with Fsui-tang for a while? Mr. Goodey and I want to have a talk."

Mickey slunk toward the bedroom, giving me unclean looks, and closed the door firmly behind him. He knew who belonged in my apartment.

Fong walked into the kitchen—my kitchen—and put the percolator over a gas burner. "You'll have some coffee?" he called over his shoulder.

"Yeah," I said, sitting down on my couch and picking up a Chinese magazine from the old coffee table some nut had made by encrusting a door with seashells, buttons, bits of glass, and other rubbish.

Fong came out of the kitchen with two cups of coffee. "It's quite a surprise to see you back so soon, Mr. Goodey."

"I can imagine," I said. "You're a bit of a surprise yourself." He laughed shyly and looked down at his clothes.

"Oh," he said, "these are my work clothes."

"I thought you were a theology student, not a cowboy," I said, but he didn't look like a cowboy, either, despite the high-heeled, tooled leather boots he was wearing.

"I am, Mr. Goodey," he said. "I am. But the biggest part of my ministry is here in the streets of North Beach." He hunched himself a little closer to me and took a tight grip on his coffee cup. I was in for a lecture. So I took a deep swig of coffee and leaned back.

"You see, Mr. Goodey," he started, "I—"

"Call me Joe," I said. "It's a lot less syllables."

"All right, Joe," he said. "And you call me Gabe." I promised with my eyes, and he went on. "You see, for the first time the Chinese population of San Francisco is faced with a serious problem—what you might call a generation gap. Chinese families have traditionally been very close, very patriarchal. And the children have, quite happily, I think, remained subordinate to their parents until they were old enough to start their own families. Chinese juvenile delinquents were almost unheard of."

What he said made sense. In fifteen years on the force I'd seen very few Chinese lads in trouble, and I'd never arrested one myself. "But," I said, to get him started again.

"But recently," he said, "the youth of Chinatown seem to have changed. They seem to have lost respect for their parents and the old ways. They're breaking away from the family, going out on their own, and getting into all kinds of trouble: crime, drugs, exploitation by adults."

"Just like white kids, eh?" I said.

He grinned shyly. "Yes, just like white kids. But my mission, Mr.—Joe, is to see if I can help the ones who will let me."

"Like little Lotus Bud there in my bed?" I asked.

"Yes. Fsui-tang. That's all I know about her—her name. But it's obvious that somebody's been using her very badly. Mickey brought her to me last night. I met him down on Grant Avenue last week, but he told me what to do with myself in no uncertain terms. I didn't want to push it too hard, so I left him alone. But last night the bell rang, and there he was—with Fsui-tang. He brought her in only after I promised that there'd be no police, no doctor, no anybody. I'd appreciate it, Joe, if you'd promise not to tell anybody that you saw her here."

"That's easy," I said. "I'm rarely asked if I've seen a teenaged Chinese dope fiend. What's wrong with her, anyway? I mean, besides the bad habit of sticking needles in her arm?"

"Nothing, so far as I can tell," Fong said. "I'm no doctor, but

I think she's just exhausted. She's been asleep most of the time since Mickey brought her here. We'll have to see after she wakes up."

"How do you know he's not her pimp?" I asked, "and has just brought her around here for a nice rest?"

"I don't," he said, but I could see that the idea hurt him. "Even if that's so, it's what I'm here for—to help girls like her and boys like Mickey."

"Good luck," I said. "But if you turn your back, don't be surprised to find a knife in it."

Fong didn't say anything, just looked sad at my cynicism. "And," I said, "there's another small problem. As you may have noticed, I seem to be back. My plans for the next six months have changed somewhat. But, in spite of this, I do remember signing Lum Kee's subletting contract, which I am positive is watertight, not to say hermetically sealed. Nonetheless—"

"Oh, I wouldn't think of holding you to that, Joe," Fong said with a big smile. "It wouldn't be a Christian thing to do." I could have argued with that statement, but I was too relieved not to find myself homeless.

"However," Fong went on, "you can understand that I need a place to stay too." He looked hopeful. "Do you think it's possible, Joe, that we could share the apartment while I'm at the Bible College?"

"You mean you, me and these underaged bandits you drag off the street?" I asked.

"Sometimes, maybe," he said. "But I don't plan to turn this into a boarding house for delinquents as a regular thing. When Fsui-tang is stronger, I'll have to find someplace for her to live."

"Where? And how soon?"

"I haven't any idea," he said. He gave me that hopeful smile again. "But in the meantime, do you think you could use the smaller bedroom? I noticed that there's an old single bed in there. Mickey and Lee could help me set it up, and—"

"Lee? Who the hell is Lee?"

"A friend of Mickey's from Grant Avenue," Fong said. "He helps Mickey take care of Fsui-tang."

"Yeah," I said. "The small room will be fine for me. I expect to be pretty busy for a while and might not be using it all that much anyway."

"That's great," he said with relief. "If it's okay with you, we'll split the rent fifty-fifty. I was a bit worried about paying the whole $225 myself anyway."

"Two twenty-five," I said. "Do you mean that old bastard is trying to charge you two hundred and twenty-five bucks a month for this joint? His own nephew?"

"That's what he said. Why?"

"Because the rent of this apartment is $130 a month. That's why. No more. That makes your share $65, plus gas and electricity. And phone. You just give me the $65, and I'll take care of your revered uncle."

"That'll be just fine with me," said Fong. "It really was deplorable of Uncle Lum to raise the rent on me."

"Deplorable is not the word I would have used. But you just leave Shylock to me. I'll sort him out."

Time was passing, and I wasn't any closer to starting to find out who had punctured Tina D'Oro. I didn't think I'd find out in this nest of tiny Chinese delinquents, so I told Fong I'd see him around and left the apartment. There was somebody named Irma—Miss Irma Springler—who, I thought, might be interesting to have a talk with.

I came down the front steps, intending to walk over to Broadway and Columbus. I pointed my nose in that direction, but as I was passing Lum Kee's shop, I heard a loud hissing noise. I knew it wasn't me, so I looked in through the doorway.

There was the old crook himself lurking in the shadows and sounding like a leaking gas main.

"Sssssss, Mr. Goodey," he said, making a beckoning motion. "One moment, please. Come in, come in."

He hadn't called me Mr. Goodey since he'd decided I wasn't needed anymore, and I'd decided I still liked the apartment. "What do you want, you old bandit?" I asked, walking into the shop. Lum Kee was standing behind the counter, wringing his hands like the mother in *East Lynne*. He was obviously suffering great mental pain, I was pleased to see.

"Mr. Goodey, Mr. Goodey," he moaned, "I'm so glad to see you back. You must help me. That nephew of mine."

"What about him?" I asked, prolonging the torture.

"He's trying to ruin me," the old fraud crooned, "filling my lovely apartment with the dregs of Grant Avenue. Drug addicts, prostitutes, gangsters. You must help me get him out. I'll do anything you say. I'll even reduce your rent if only you'll help me."

"How much will you cut my rent if I give Fong the bum's rush?" I wanted to find out just how anxious Lum was.

His bright little eyes clouded over with cunning. I could almost hear the figures brushing past one another as they tumbled through his head.

"If it will help," I said, "I'll wait while you go get your abacus." He didn't even hear me. The magic subject of money had wafted him to a different, higher plane. But he was coming back again, and he fixed me with an eager look.

"Ten dollars a month," he said as if he were offering me the Kohinoor diamond, gift wrapped. "I'll cut your rent to $120 a month if you persuade my nephew to move somewhere else. That's a very good deal, Mr. Goodey. An apartment like that—those marvelous views—is worth at least—"

"Two twenty-five?" I asked. "Do you think that would be a

fair rent to charge, say, someone from out of town, someone from across the sea who didn't know what a rotten little fleabag like that was worth? Let's say a not-so-distant relative who'd come to San Francisco to become a man of God."

Lum Kee's mouth went hard. He knew I had tumbled his little con. He didn't say anything, just crossed his flabby old arms across his ink-stained black vest and stared at me.

"Honestly, Lum Kee," I said, "I could understand you trying to cheat me, not only an infidel dog but a copper. But to try to do your own sister Pansy's youngest boy, that really shocks me."

"One fifteen," he said, cutting through my bullshit in the only language he trusted, "and I'll paint the whole apartment for you. That's my bottom offer."

"Don't tempt me to tell you what to do with your bottom offer, Lum Kee," I said. "The kid stays, and you get the same old $130 a month. If he wants to raise turkeys up there, it's okay by me. I'll take that extra ninety-five bucks you charged him out of next month's rent, and if you think you can get any place waving that phony contract around, go ahead and try it."

I left him leaning against his counter, making a mouth like a broken piggy bank, and started walking downhill toward Broadway. I didn't expect Lum to accept defeat gracefully, but he'd be quiet for a while, thinking up a counterattack. God knows what he'd come up with next. Maybe a typhoid epidemic.

8

It was getting well on toward evening as I reached Broadway and turned toward the hub of North Beach. At that hour the whores and other starlets were having breakfast; the pimps, who'd been up and hustling for at least three hours, were having lunch; and the honest citizens, who'd just closed their shops, were having dinner. Ranked in doorways in side streets, the Tokay Brigade was augmenting its liquid diet with more liquid.

At The Jungle, a retired hubcap thief in an oversized doorman's coat was shooing black kids away from the display pictures out front. Tina's name was still on the marquee in eighteen-inch letters with the word tonight! There was a lot of sentiment on North Beach. A lot of heart.

"Business as usual, eh?" I asked the doorman.

"Huh?" he said, aiming a last sharp-toed kick at one of the dodging kids.

"Is Fat Phil around?"

The doorman, a man of few words, jerked a dirty thumb

toward the interior of The Jungle and went back to examining his life for the exact moment he'd gone wrong.

I started to push open the door but then paused.

"Too bad about Tina," I said.

"Huh?" he said.

"If you can perfect that routine," I told him, "you'll be up on the stage inside instead of bruising your insteps out here." I went in and closed the double door behind me before he could get off his famous rejoinder. He could wear out that act if he didn't watch it.

The inside of The Jungle looked like a bad interior for *Tarzan Goes on the Bottle*. But then I suppose darkness and seven or eight watered drinks would lend a certain amount of verisimilitude to the tired plastic foliage and stuffed animals. Up over the bar was the tiny jungle clearing where Tina had done most of her shaking. But she'd swung on her last vine.

In front of the bar, taking up two stools and part of a third was Fat Phil Franks, front man for The Jungle and Tina's former manager. It had made big headlines in San Francisco late last year when Tina and Phil had split the managerial blanket. It doesn't take much to make headlines in San Francisco. But she'd stayed on at The Jungle. Phil had lost his fifteen percent, and now he'd lost his headliner.

I walked up to the back of his neck—a flabby tree trunk with a five-dollar haircut—and said: "It's kind of you, Phil, to keep Tina's name up in lights. She'd have been all choked up at that kind of sentiment."

Instead of waiting for him to turn around—that could have taken all evening at the rate he moved his three hundred and seventy-five pounds—I moved up to the bar to his right where he could swivel his neck at me without doing any serious damage to his system. I allowed him three or four bar stools for overflow and took a seat.

"Oh, hi," he said. "Yeah, I thought it was the least I could do for poor Tina. I'm leaving her up there until after the funeral—as a mark of respect."

"When's that?"

"Tomorrow afternoon," he said.

"You going?"

"If I can," he said sadly. "But you know how hard it is for me to get around. I'd really like to. I wasn't even able to go up to her place when they found her." With his weight and over-worked heart, Phil hadn't been above the ground floor of any building since he'd topped three hundred pounds. "But I'm sending a blanket of three thousand gardenias to the funeral. From me and The Jungle."

"Touching," I said. "But tell me something. How can you leave Tina's name on the marquee and not give the suckers any Tina? Don't they get irate when they're getting some second stringer instead?"

Fat Phil parted his face in a smile that would have been terrifying on a man half his size. "Movies," he said. "The best of Tina D'Oro in sixteen-millimeter living color. Wide screen."

"You're a genius, Phil," I said. "How long do you think you can get away with that?"

"Long enough," he said, taking a long slurp of something vile and sickly from a tall glass, "for me to get my replacement for Tina ready to go on stage. God forbid I should speak ill of the dead, Joe," he said, "but this girl is going to make Tina look like a cub scout."

"That's wonderful," I said. "You're going to be the fattest millionaire in the world. But I didn't come here to watch you turn Tina's death into your next fortune. I'm trying to locate someone called Irma Springler. A friend of Tina's. Do you know where I can find her?"

"You working on this case?" he asked, his dark-chocolate

eyes growing wise. "I would have thought that after zapping Kolchik's cousin you'd be low man on the sewers squad."

"You'll think a lot of things before you're done, Phil," I said. I leaned over toward him and got confidential. "Don't tell a soul, but I'm up for promotion. The mayor never did like his cousin. He thanked me personally for perforating the old geezer. If I'd been just a little better shot, I'd be a captain right this minute."

"Sure," Phil said. "Right after I win the Kentucky Derby. On foot. What were we talking about?"

"Irma Springler."

"I've seen her around," Phil said. "What do you want to talk to her about?"

"Things, Phil," I said. "Just things. I'm enjoying this chat an awful lot, but unless you can be just a bit more helpful, I'm going to have to go outside and talk with a lamppost. Do you know one that might know where Irma Springler lives?"

"Well," he said, "she lives over on Union—the 400 block—but I don't think she's home now."

"Let me take the risk. I can handle it. But the 400 block of Union is quite long, Phil. Do you think you could narrow it down a little?"

"It's either 416 or 461," he said. "But you're wasting your time going over there."

"I can afford it," I said. "Don't get up. I'll see myself out." I left him working hard over that tall glass. Just before I opened the door, I stopped and leaned toward his massive back. "By the way, Phil," I said, "you don't have any idea who killed Tina, do you?"

If he answered, I didn't hear it.

Phil was right. Number 461 turned out to be a Victorian shambles with a slight lean toward Russian Hill, and a postbox name plate said "I. Springler, 4B." He was right on another

count. After I puffed up four steep flights and leaned on the
bell of 4B, nobody answered. I clouted the door a couple of
times in case I. Springler was a little deaf. But all that got me
was a sour look from her neighbor in 4C, a stringy old lady with
the long lower lip and sparse beard of a nanny goat, who leaned
out of her door and gave me a high, hard one out of her
good eye.

"You looking for someone?" she quavered.

"Just Irma Springler," I said. "Have you seen her today?"
"No."

"Have you seen her this week?"

"No."

I was going to try for this month, but I knew the answer I'd
get and I wasn't ready to go to a year.

"Thanks very much," I said. "If you do see Miss Springler,
would you..." The door shut with an emphatic crunch.

It was easier going down, and by the time I got downstairs it
was dark. It was a nice night for walking home. Broadway was
kicking into life as I passed through. Club-door barkers were
trying out their lines of lapel-grabbing innuendo, and dudes
from Cotati, Burlingame, and El Cerrito sidled down the street,
avoiding the doormen's blandishments and looking for that
mythical club where the drinks weren't watered and they were
taking it all off right there in front of your face.

Back on my block, all was peaceful. The door to Lum Kee's
shop was shut, locked, barred, and probably booby-trapped.

A glance up at my apartment's lighted windows told me
that somebody was home to welcome me. It had been quite a
while since there'd been a light on for me, and the idea was
cheering. I flipped on the stairway lamp and started climbing.

I usually climb stairs looking at my feet, but something up
ahead on the second landing caught my eye. It was Chub, my
old buddy, sitting on the top step, fat hands piled in his lap, like

an Occidental Buddha. His round eyes were peacefully closed, and I thought Chub had dozed off waiting for me until I saw the thin line of blood running from the left side of his mouth down over those well-fed chops onto the front of his mohair suit.

That is, it had been a stream of blood, but as I got closer I could see that it had dried to a ribbon of rusty red. "Chub," I said, the way people will talk to a dead man, and I touched his unbloodied shoulder. His plump little body rocked, and I had to stop him from tumbling forward. He'd been precariously balanced in death, and I'd upset that balance. Moving a hand to his back, I started to lay him down on the landing. My hand found a sticky patch of blood between his shoulder blades and came away gory, but I got him laid down. His knees were still slightly bent, and in the harsh light of the landing I half expected Chub to throw a hand up to shield his eyes.

When I opened the door of my apartment, Fong was sitting on the long, green couch going over some printed forms. The door to my bedroom—my former bedroom—was closed, so I assumed that Mickey was in there playing Florence Nightingale to the girl junkie.

"Hello, Joe," Fong said. "Fsui-tang woke up a while ago and is resting comfortably. I really do think she was just worn out."

"I hope she's well enough for company," I said, washing my hands at the kitchen sink, "because we're going to have some soon. There's a dead man lying on the next landing down, and I've got to call the police."

"A dead man?" Fong said right on cue. "But who? Are you sure he's dead?" He was up off the couch, prepared to do something Christian.

"I'm sure," I said. "I've seen one before. Do you remember that little man who was here yesterday when you came up to see the apartment?"

"Yes. You called him—"

"Chub, but his name was Seymour Kroll. Somebody stuck something very much like a knife in Mr. Kroll's back not too long ago. And from the blood on the stairs, I'd say it happened right outside the door of this apartment. I don't suppose you heard anything?"

"No. And I've been here since you left. I—"

"Save it for homicide," I said, reaching over to pick up the telephone. "You'd better warn your delinquents in the next room that the police are coming. They may not want to stay."

I was right. No sooner had I told a very alert and cheerful sergeant about Chub's accident than the door to the bedroom opened and Mickey came out carrying the girl. He was only a little devil, but she looked as though she weighed about as much as a box of Wheaties. Fong followed them, still trying to talk Mickey into staying. He wasn't having much luck.

"Thanks, Gabe," said Mickey, "but we're not going to be here when the cops come. I'll get in touch in a few days. We'll be all right." The girl wasn't saying anything. She was conscious, and eyes the color of a moonless night took in the small room. She lay back in Mickey's arms like a failed channel swimmer.

It occurred to me that I still had the file on Tina D'Oro and that it wouldn't be a great idea for the police to find me with it. I got an idea.

"Can your boy here be trusted?" I asked Fong.

"Sure," said Fong. "I think so."

"Okay." I pulled out a pen and wrote my name and an address on the envelope the records came in and sealed it. I put a couple of postage stamps in the corner and put the envelope and a five-dollar bill on top of Fsui-tang.

"Do me a favor," I said. "Drop this in the first postbox you come to."

"Okay," said Mickey. "We're off."

Then they were gone, and I could hear Mickey's heavy shoes clunk down the thin-carpeted stairs. He slowed right about where Chub's body would have been, but then picked up speed again. From my front window I saw them leave the building and disappear between two fences across the narrow street.

Their short shadow had hardly disappeared when a prowl car swung in off Jackson and climbed the curb in front of the building. Two uniformed cops sprang out of the car and clanked across the sidewalk into the building. We'd be seeing more of those boys. "What shall we do?" asked Fong.

"Wait. It won't take them long to get up here."

"No, I mean about Mickey and Fsui-tang," he said. "Shall we tell the police they were here but left? Won't they be angry?"

"Very likely," I said. "But it's usually the best policy to tell the police the truth. Unless you have a good reason not to. Do you know where those two kids have gone?"

"No."

"Then you can't very well tell the police, can you?" I asked. "So I think we'd better tell it the way it happened. Okay?"

Before he could answer, somebody hit the door with what sounded like a baked ham, and I gestured for Fong to answer the door. When he did, the doorway was full of blue serge, and a cop started to ask if Fong was the guy who reported a dead body. Then he looked over Fong's shoulder and saw me.

"Goodey!" he said. "What the hell are you doing here?" It was Gerry Anderson, a thick-skulled Swede I'd soldiered with a long time ago in the Parks Division. He hadn't been too happy when I got into plainclothes.

"I live here," I said. "And I reported finding the body. This is the Reverend Gabriel Fong. He shares this place with me."

Anderson looked Fong's urban guerrilla outfit up and down and wondered whether to call me a liar. But after a lot of soul-searching—he did everything but take off his hat and give himself a Dutch rub—he decided not to chance it. That's why Anderson was still in uniform and always would be.

"Who's the dude down on the landing?" Anderson wanted to know.

"His name is Seymour Kroll," I said. "He's a lawyer's investigator from New York. I found him about twelve minutes ago sitting on the landing, leaking a bit of blood. When I touched him, he fell over, and I let him lie."

"You didn't disturb—" Anderson began, but then he thought better of it.

"I didn't anything," I told him. "So why don't we just stand around and talk about old times until the experts get here?"

Anderson didn't like that remark, but, lacking a better one, he stood glowering at me and Fong. Mostly me.

"Say," he said, "is there anyone else here?"

Fong eyed me as I said no.

There was a half knock on the door as it was shoved open, and Anderson's partner came into the apartment. He couldn't have been over twenty-one, and he looked as if he'd taken the oath that afternoon just in time to go on shift. He was a fresh-faced kid who had success written all over him. From the way Anderson looked at him, I knew he could see it too.

"Hey, Andy," he said, "that guy..."

"I know," said Anderson. "Go down to the front door and wait for homicide. Tell them I'm up here. And check out anybody who comes in or leaves the building." He said this last bit to nobody, because the kid had already gone.

Anderson amused himself by opening doors and peering into the other rooms of the apartment while Fong and I exchanged assorted glances.

"Too bad about the old watchman," Anderson said by way of time-passing conversation. What he meant as a cop was "too bad you pulled a bad one." As a cop I understood him exactly. "Hope it doesn't come down too hard on you." Apparently news of my departure from the force hadn't sunk to the lowest levels.

"Me too," I said honestly, not giving away a thing.

This brilliant exchange was interrupted by a thumping of feet up the stairs, and the young cop burst in through the door followed by Johnny Maher. Detective Sergeant Johnny Maher.

Johnny wasn't that much older than the rookie—maybe five years—but in true age he could have been the boy's grandfather. There were ages behind those pale-green eyes, ages of deprivation and downgrading that he was in a hurry to make up for. Johnny was a sharp-dressing cop. Not rich, but sharp. You'd never have mistaken him for a bank president.

Or a pimp. If you guessed a pro football quarterback or a local-TV chat-show host, you'd be close to his style. Right then, his style was direct. "What's going on here, Goodey?" he asked. He used to call me Joe, but that was earlier in the week before he'd made sergeant.

"A little murder, Johnny," I said, "or so it seems. I was just telling Andy here that the victim was a friend of mine, a lawyer's investigator out from New York."

Up until that moment Maher hadn't given any indication that he'd been aware of Anderson's existence. He was like that with the troops and was famous as Maher the Patrolman's Friend. "Anyone else here?" He threw the question at Andy as you'd throw a dog a poisoned bone.

"Not since I been here," Anderson said through his big, pale-gray teeth.

"Well, take your young friend here out and find out what

the neighbors know," said Johnny. "You won't get much done holding up the walls here."

The two men in uniform went out, Anderson seething and the youngster half-admiring Maher but making a mental note to be nicer to patrolmen when he was a detective sergeant. Maher and I stood silently looking at each other.

"Nice going, Johnny," I said. "You've made another good buddy among the peons. Andy will be your pallbearer when some other cop zaps you."

"I'm not paid to be chummy with the troops, Goodey," Maher said. "I do my job and I see that they do theirs. And, speaking of jobs, I understand you've had a recent change of employment." The word was trickling out. "Sort of, Johnny," I said. "I decided to go to work for a living."

All this time Gabriel Fong had been sitting in my old easy chair, watching us as if we were characters in a lousy play. I hate to say it, but the expression on his face was inscrutable. I liked to think that he didn't care for Maher because I disliked him. But they might have turned out to be the best of pals. Might have.

But the next thing Johnny did was arch a nearly double-jointed thumb in Fong's direction and ask, "Who's that?"

I started to open my mouth, but Fong beat me to it. "That," he said, "is the cotenant of this apartment you've just barged into without invitation." The voice was tougher than I'd have thought possible. "Who are you? I assume that you're a police officer, but I've seen no proof."

Maher gave me an eyebrow-lifting look, as if he expected me to intervene just short of throwing Fong out of the window, but I sat still and did nothing.

Like a quick-draw artist, Maher went into his inside coat pocket and came out with his leather badge holder, which he right-jabbed under Fong's snub nose. To read it, Fong would have had to go cross-eyed.

"That satisfy you?" Maher snarled.

Fong reached up, effortlessly pushed the badge-holding hand out to reading distance, and read it slowly, not missing any of the small print. That's my boy.

"Thank you, sergeant," he said mildly. "My name is Gabriel Fong. I'm a theological student at the San Francisco Bible College, and I live here. Is there anything else you want to know?"

"Yeah," said Maher. But just then heavy feet thumped up the stairs, and Andy came in through the half-open door, trying not to look too excited.

"Sergeant," he said, puffing a little, "an old lady across the street says just before we got here somebody suspicious left in a hurry. A Chinese kid, and it looked like he was carrying a little girl. She doesn't know where they went."

Maher wheeled on me and Fong. "You know anything about this?" he demanded.

"Yes," I said. "They were here until I found Kroll's body, but then they remembered they had a date somewhere. So they left."

Maher wasn't the exploding type. His face turned to stone. "Goodey," he said quietly, "are you telling me that you let two potential suspects leave here after you knew a murder had been committed?"

"That's right," I said easily. "I had no right to stop them. I'm not a cop anymore." I didn't bother going into the unlikelihood of a sick girl and her volunteer nurse sneaking out into the hall and knifing Chub. Anderson was having enough problems with the first bit of information I'd dropped. He kept boggling and looked as though he was wondering who to slug.

Maher took it quite well. Too well, in fact. "Right," he said smoothly, "you're not a cop anymore. But you are a suspect, and so are you, Charlie Chan." He whipped a pair of cuffs out of his back pocket and flipped them to Anderson.

"Tie these monkeys together, Andy," he said. "Frisk them and take them downtown. Have them put in detention until I get there, and then come right back."

"You haven't read us Miranda," I said, anxious that Maher shouldn't do anything to imperil his new stripes.

"Fuck Miranda," he said. "You know it, and you can explain it to your friend in the lockup."

"You see," I told Fong, "there's nothing to worry about. Cops like Maher only skip the finer legal points when they don't expect an arrest to stick. He's pissed because we let Mickey and Fsui-tang leave."

"Cuffs!" snapped Maher.

Relieved to have something to do, Andy did an expert job of cuffing me to Gabriel and then himself to me. He had to be good at something.

"It's the city's gasoline," I told Maher as Anderson started tugging us out the door, "but you're wasting it. Do you know who Mr. Fong is?"

Maher signaled for Andy to stop. "I'll bite," he said. "Who is Mr. Fong?"

"The mayor's cousin. His *other* cousin."

Maher didn't even bother to respond to that. He just thumbed Andy and us out the door.

Andy didn't have a lot to say on the way down to headquarters. Neither did Fong and I, but there in the caged-in back seat we got in a few whispers.

"What will happen now, Joe?" Fong asked.

"They'll lock us up for a little while," I said. "But don't worry. I'll have us out within a couple of hours."

"I hope you're right," he said. So did I.

9

IF YOU THINK THE AVERAGE LAW-ABIDING CITIZEN FEELS strange finding himself in a cell, imagine how a cop feels. It's not natural. It's like a dog being peed on by a lamppost. I'd known Archie Meltzer, the chief turnkey on duty, for over ten years, but you wouldn't have known it from the way he processed me for the cells.

"Hello, Archie," I said in a friendly way.

"Empty out all your pockets," said Archie. "Put your money, car keys, other valuables on the table."

"Sure, Archie," I said, turning out my pockets. "How's your kid brother? He still racing those pigeons?"

"Remove your belt, tie, if any, and shoelaces," Archie said, "and place them on the table next to the long, brown envelope." Another turnkey I didn't know was busy counting the money we'd put on the table and making an itemized list of the other things.

"Right," I said. "You know best. But, Archie, there is one thing. I'd kind of like to make that telephone call. You know, the one everybody talks about. It's important."

"Plenty of time for that later," said Archie, "Read the itemized list, initial each entry and sign your accustomed signature
and the date at the bottom." We'd done all this like good boys,
and Archie was telling his helper where to stash us. "Okay," he
said, deadpan, "this way."

"Archie," I said, "I don't want to be a nag, but I'd really like
to make that phone call. And my friend, Mr. Fong, would probably like to make one, too. It is the law, you know."

"I know the law, Joe," Archie said, using my name for the
first time, "and you'll get your phone call. Now, do as the man
says." I did as the man said, leading Fong through the green,
metal door and down the corridor that leads to the dozen or so
cells where drunks and other master criminals were kept.
There were also a couple of high-security cells, and I wondered
if I had enough status to get one of those.

The turnkey stopped us in front of a cell with a guy already
in it and opened the door. "Not you," he said as I started to go
in. "You." He motioned to Fong.

"Don't despair, Gabe," I said. "I'll have us out of here in no
time."

"Sure, Joe," he said, but he didn't sound too sure. I didn't
feel too sure. As the turnkey was locking Fong in, his new roommate, a little whey-faced guy with a dirty-blond pompadour
and the eyes of a child molester, came to the front bars and
stared at me.

"What did you do?" I asked him just to pass the time.

"I got caught," he said.

The turnkey prodded me on down the line to an empty cell
and opened the door. As I stepped in, he clanged the door shut
behind me.

"Hey," I said, turning, "tell Archie that unless..." But he
was already halfway down the row and gaining speed. "You'll
be sorry," I said, but I couldn't think how.

It wasn't much of a cell. Two steel cots bolted to the floor, a chemical toilet in the corner. On each cot was a thin, striped mattress and a folded war-surplus blanket. Mine had been in the Navy. The walls of the cell were solid concrete with close-set bars starting about six feet up and going to the ceiling on each side. High at the back was a barred ventilator grate.

I sat down and wondered how long it would take Archie to get around to letting me make my phone call. I also wondered who had knifed Chub and whether it had anything to do with the little job I was supposed to be doing for Kolchik. Suppose Kolchik murdered Chub. These heavy thoughts were interrupted by a sound from overhead.

"Sssssssssss!"

I looked up and saw a small, black face looking down at me from just where the bars began above the concrete wall. On either side of the face were two, thin-fingered hands, pink on one side, black on the other.

"Sssssss!" the face repeated.

"Yeah?" I said.

"Shhhhhhh!" my sibilant neighbor said. "Shhhhhh! Come up here for a minute, but keep your voice down."

I didn't have much else to do, so I stood up on the other bunk. "What do you want?" I whispered.

"What are you in for?" He looked like a teenager.

"Suspicion of murder," I said. I tried to be matter-of-fact, but it wasn't easy.

"Wow! You don't look like a murderer."

"I'm not," I admitted. "It's a bum rap. I'll be out of here in a little while." I said that to encourage myself as much as anything.

"You look like a pretty good guy," my neighbor said. "Will you do me a favor?"

"I'll try. What is it?"

"I want you to tell the jailer something for me. I've tried, but he won't listen to me."

"He's not doing an awful lot of listening to me, either. But I'll give it a try. What is it?"

He pushed his pointed little face up until his nose was between the bars and glanced nervously behind him at the other bunk in the cell.

"I'm a girl," my neighbor whispered. "I shouldn't be in this part of the jail. I got picked up for vagrancy, and I wasn't going to tell them 'cause I thought they'd put me in a cell by myself and I'd get out in the morning. But they put me in here with him—" We both looked at the bunk on the far wall. Beneath a gently rising and falling blanket was what looked like an escaped gorilla. A cruel face was relaxed in dreamless sleep. I'm positive the slack lips covered long fangs.

"I'm afraid that, once he wakes up, he'll find out I'm a girl and..."

I'd have been afraid to have been in that cell when it woke up too.

"I'll do what I can," I whispered. "But what are you doing dressed up like a boy?"

She shrugged and gave me a sharp-toothed little smile. "It happens," she said. "You just tell that jailer to get me out of here and do it quick and quiet. Okay?"

"Okay," I said. "I'll do it just as soon as I can, but—"

Behind her, Mighty Joe Young stirred noisily, threw out a hand the size of a seven-dollar sirloin and brought it back to shield its eyes from the light in the corridor. "Humph," it growled. "Too fuckin' noisy in here."

My neighbor dropped like a hanged man—woman—and I heard the bedsprings squeaking as she burrowed underneath the bedding.

I dropped down on my side and sat down again. If I

couldn't get Archie to listen to my story, how could I tell him about my lady neighbor? I didn't even have a tin cup to rattle on the bars. That problem was solved when the turnkey came padding along the corridor and stopped in front of my cell. He unlocked the door.

"Come on," he said. "Archie says you can make that telephone call now."

I jumped up and walked out of the cell. As I walked past the next cell, I heard a tiny whisper: "Don't forget." King Kong was snoring once again.

When I came into the turnkey's office, Archie gestured gracefully toward the telephone on his desk. "There you go, Joe," he said. "One call."

"Thanks loads. You're a credit to law enforcement."

I considered calling the mayor, just to make Archie and his flunky drop their teeth. But I didn't know his number and thought maybe it wouldn't be such a cool thing to do. So I dialed a certain number in Mill Valley.

"Lehman," said a voice full of mashed potatoes.

"Goodey," I said, pausing slightly, "speaking from the city jail, where at present I'm an unwilling guest."

"Joe," Ralph asked, "what the hell are you up to? I'm eating dinner right now, and we've got guests."

"I've got guests, too," I said. "Two lovely jailers standing here listening to every word I say. And I haven't had any dinner at all." I turned my head toward Archie. "What's for dinner tonight, Arch?"

"Too late, Joe," he said. "You've missed it."

"The man says I've missed dinner," I told Ralph, "so I suggest that you get down here and get me out before I tell everything I know for a ham sandwich."

"But Joe," said Lehman, "what are you in jail for? At least tell me that."

"Suspicion of murder," I said. "Johnny Maher thinks I killed somebody this evening."

"Killed somebody?"

"Yeah. And not who you think. Somebody else."

"Where's Maher right now?"

"At my place, as far as I know, pinning everything on me. But I wouldn't be surprised to find him paying me a visit down here in a little while."

"Just hold tight, Joe," Ralph said. "I'll be right there. Don't worry about a thing."

"I'm not worried," I said. "I've got great faith in you."

"One thing," he said. "Do those jailers know who you're calling?"

"I'll ask." I put my hand over the speaker. "Say, do you lads have any idea who I'm talking to?"

They shook their heads.

"Nope," I said. "For all they know, you could be the Pope."

"Good," he said. "I'll be down to get you out right away, but if you let on that you expect me, I'll leave you in the cells until you rot."

"Right," I said. "See you around." I hung up.

"Okay," said Archie. "Back you go." The other turnkey opened the door of the office.

"Wait a minute," I said. "Archie, I'll do a deal with you. I'll tell you something you want to know if your man here will go out and get me a sandwich and a cup of coffee. And a candy bar."

"What sort of thing I want to know?" Very suspicious.

"Something you're going to be very embarrassed about if I don't tell you."

"What is it?" Archie asked. I knew I had him hooked.

"Oh, no. I want your promise first. Sandwich—make it

pastrami and Swiss cheese on an onion roll—black coffee, and a Hershey bar…it's a good deal, Archie. You better take it."

He chewed on it a bit and then said: "It's a deal. Spill it."

"Okay," I said. "I know your word is your bond. You know those two guys in the cell next to mine—the one closest to this office?"

"Yes. The two spades. What about them?"

"One of them's a girl."

"A girl? In my jail?"

"That's right. Not the caveman, but the little, pointy-chinned one. She told me just before your man brought me in."

"Harvey," Archie said, "get that girl out of there, get her out fast and get her out quietly. Put Joe back in—and then get him something to eat."

"Don't forget the mustard on the pastrami, Harv," I said. "Lots of it."

I was just licking the melted chocolate from my fingers when Harvey came back to my cell and stuck the key in the lock.

"Just in time, Harvey," I said. "I always like a little walk after dinner."

"That's good," he said, "but you're not walking where you think. You're going upstairs. I don't think that lawyer of yours got the message."

"Ah, well," I said, "he's only human. Who'm I going to see, then?"

"You'll find out."

As we passed through the turnkey's office, Archie was sitting at his green, metal desk. He still looked worried.

"Did you take care of my girlfriend?" I asked.

"Son of a bitch, Joe," he said. "In nineteen years I never had such a thing happen. You can't tell them apart these days. You just can't tell."

"Serves you right, Archie, for being so nasty to me when I came in here this evening. Take good care of my man Fong. I'll be back for him in a little while."

Archie just looked sicker, and Harvey nudged me to get moving. The fifth floor was dark and empty except for Lehman's office. Ralph was sitting behind his desk looking half-fed and pissed off. "Thanks, Winston," he told my guide. "I'll take over now. You sit down, Goodey." After Harvey had closed the door behind him, Ralph looked up at me: "Why, Joe, why? I gave you a perfectly simple job, an important job. And what happens?"

"I didn't ask for the job," I pointed out.

He ignored me. "Somebody," he said, "somebody you might have had a reasonably good reason to kill, gets knocked off on your doorstep. And now I've got to get you out of jail."

"Your buddy, Maher, got me put into jail," I said. "He knows I didn't kill Seymour Kroll."

"Who did then?" Lehman asked.

"You got me," I said. "Maybe the same person who knocked off Tina."

"But why?"

"Beats me," I said. "You have any idea what the mayor was doing early this evening?"

Lehman looked too weary even to reply to that and was saved the trouble when there was a bang on the door which might have been mistaken for a knock, and Johnny Maher came charging in, looking less than happy.

"Ralph," he said, "what the hell—"

"Sit down, Johnny," Lehman said, gesturing toward a chair across from mine.

"But, Ralph—"

"SIT DOWN!" Ralph shouted, all but blowing Johnny toward the chair, where he settled unhappily but quietly.

"Now, listen to me, Maher," Ralph said evenly but menacingly enough. "As of right now you've got nothing to do with that murder at Goodey's place."

"Outside Goodey's place," I insisted.

"Shut up, Goodey," Ralph said. Maher liked that, but he wasn't so cheerful when Ralph swiveled toward him and continued, "I don't know how you got the job in the first place."

"Nobody else was there to handle it," said Maher sullenly.

"Well, there will be, starting right now, if I have to do it myself. As for you, haven't you got enough to do with the D'Oro stabbing? I think you're aware that the mayor would like that little matter settled—and soon."

Maher looked like a kid caught with unfinished homework.

"By the way," Lehman plunged on, "how are you doing on the D'Oro case? Have you anything to report?"

"Not yet," said Maher, casting a sideways look at me. "I haven't been able to locate the Springler woman yet, but I will. There's not too much to work on, but I'll come up with the answer. Don't worry."

"I do worry," said Lehman sharply. "I worry about retiring next year on two thirds of my lousy pay. I worry about you keeping those three stripes you so cleverly won. I hope you haven't bothered to sew them on, because if you don't settle this D'Oro case and do it soon, you won't have them long. Now, get out of here and accomplish something. And stay away from Goodey. He's bad luck." Maher fled without a glance at me.

"Thanks, Ralph," I said.

"Don't thank me," he said. "I didn't do anything for you. I was giving it to Maher straight. I want results, and I want them yesterday. But first, how does this latest murder fit in?"

"Maybe it doesn't," I said, "but it certainly makes life more interesting. What time is it? Those guys downstairs have my watch, and I've got to call someone in New York and tell him about the demise of Seymour Kroll."

"It's nine-thirty. Who are you going to call?"

"My father-in-law. But it's after midnight there. I might wait until morning. Kroll won't be any deader then."

"Well, then," Lehman said, "if it's not too much trouble, can we talk about the D'Oro case for a minute?"

"Yeah," I said. "After all, I've been on the damned thing a whole six hours, including the time I've been in your jail. I ought to have it wrapped up by now." I put a hand toward the inside pocket of my coat. "I have the name of the murderer in this sealed envelope..."

"Okay, okay," said Ralph. "But can't we talk?"

"Sure," I said. "But first get on that phone and tell them to let Gabriel Fong go."

"Gabriel Fong?"

"That's right. F-O-N-G. Rhymes with gong. He's the guy I sublet my apartment to when you ran me out of town. He's a Bible student, and we'll be sharing the place while he takes a course here and mops up all the delinquents in Chinatown. He was with me this evening when Maher..."

"Say no more." Lehman reached for the telephone and dialed. "Archie," he said, "Chief Lehman. Have you got a guy down there called Fong? Well, let him go. Never mind what Maher says. Send him home and tell him we'll be in touch."

"And tell Archie to send my stuff up here," I said. "They have all my money."

"Oh, yes," Ralph said. "Joe Goodey will be coming back down for his effects. Don't throw him back in the cells. Okay?" He put down the receiver and swiveled back to me. "Give," he said.

"There's not much to give," I told him. But, starting from the moment that afternoon when I'd left him in Bruno's office, I gave him a rundown on my less-than-enlightening inquiries... right up to the time I'd found Chub, and Maher had found me. I even told him about the two Chinese kids.

At first Ralph didn't say anything. He just gave a big, wheezy sigh as if the thumb of God were pressing on his chest in an unfriendly way.

Then he said: "I was right, wasn't I, Joe? You should have been a private dick all the time. You're a natural. Here you've had a private op's license a full six hours or so, and you're working overtime finding dead bodies, disappearing potential murderers and witnesses, bumping heads with detective sergeants all over the place. You've got the knack, boy."

I tried to look modest, but he didn't give me much of a chance.

"But the one thing you haven't done," he went on, "is make much visible or even invisible progress toward finding out what we all want to know—who iced Tina D'Oro. Am I right?"

"You're right," I said. "But tell me something. It occurred to me while Mr. Maher was here. By any chance has he read Tina's diary? I mean beyond the point of learning that our leader was making beautiful music with Tina?"

"He says not. Maher claims that he was just flicking through idly, not reading, when he spotted Sandy's name. After that, he put it away and didn't look in it again."

"Do you believe him?"

"Not necessarily. Johnny's too smart for his own good. Time will tell. But right now isn't there something you should be out doing?"

"Yeah," I said, "there probably is."

I left him looking like part of the tired office furniture, collected my belongings from the still-shattered Archie, and again found myself standing on the sidewalk outside the police building.

10

I THOUGHT ABOUT HEADING RIGHT BACK TO NORTH Beach, nosing around, asking some questions, zeroing in on whoever did Tina in. I thought about going around and slapping the crap out of Johnny Maher, just for the fun of it. I thought about picking up one end of the Golden Gate Bridge and throwing it in the bay.

Exhausted, I headed for the friendliest thing in sight—a brightly lit, green telephone booth. I won a little argument with the booth's folding door and looked at my watch. Just after ten. After one in the morning in New York. Who said Sonny Berkowitz had a right to an undisturbed night's sleep? I had enough quarters in my pocket to invest in a cheap-rate three-minute call, and I started dialing area code 2 1 2.

The telephone on the other end rang with an annoyed rasp about seven times, and then a voice answered. I knew that voice.

"It's me—Joe," I said. "But don't hang up. I'm calling Sonny."

"Joe," said my wife in a voice permeated with wariness.

"Mom and Dad aren't here. They've gone up to the Connecticut place for the weekend. They still haven't had a telephone put in up there." Was this the siren voice that made me rush to New York and go crazy six months before? It was hard to believe. All I could hear was a slightly nasal, vaguely babyish New York voice.

"You'll have to give Sonny a message then," I said. "I've got some bad news for him. That investigator he sent out to bug me was killed tonight. Somebody stabbed him just outside the door to the apartment." I almost said "our apartment."

"Killed?" said Pat. "But why? He was such a nice little man. Why would anybody want to kill him?"

I thought I'd skip the wisecracks. "I haven't any idea, Pat," I said. "I found his body only a couple of hours ago, and the police are investigating. They'll probably find out who did it. As you may have heard somewhere, I'm not a cop anymore."

There was a small silence on her end. Pat was probably trying to decide how sympathetic she could be without taking a chance of triggering me. It was a valid question.

"Yes," she said. "Daddy told me. That was bad luck. Is the old man all right?"

"Yeah. He'll be okay."

"And you," she said cautiously, "are you okay, Joe?" She meant to convey that she was concerned but not too much.

"Sure," I said. "Never better." Keep up a brave front, Goodey.

"What are you going to do now?" she asked.

"Well, yesterday I was thinking about a little vacation in Mexico. But this morning I changed my mind. I think I'll stick around here and see what happens. It's a fairly lively place. I might take some sort of job. How about you? How are things at the agency? Still knocking them out, ad-wise?"

"I suppose so," she said. "It gets pretty hectic at times." There was a pause. "Joe—"

I knew what was coming. "Yeah?" I said warily.

"I know it seems terrible, what with Mr. Kroll just getting killed— I still can't believe it—but are you going to let me have a divorce? It's really the best thing for everybody, you know."

I heard myself saying something I hadn't planned. "Yes, Pat," I said. "I know it is. I know."

"Well, then?" she said in that logical tone of voice I used to hate. There was a long, long pause. The last five years flickered through my head like a high-speed movie.

"All right," I said. "You can have it. Send me the papers, and I'll sign them."

The line went silent again. I knew I'd surprised her. I'd surprised myself. "Are you sure, Joe?" Pat asked. I suspected that she was trying to keep the excitement out of her voice.

"Sure," I said. "Send me the papers before I change my mind. Tell Sonny that Seymour talked me into it. If there was a Mrs. Kroll, maybe he'll give her a bonus. But let's not talk about it right now. I've already got too much on my mind."

"But, Joe..."

At that point the operator came on, demanding more money for more time, and I wasn't sorry to say that I was out of quarters. So I said a quick goodbye and hung up. I wouldn't have to think about the divorce again until the papers came.

A telephone booth can be a cozy place, especially when you have no particular place to go. But it's not a way of life. I fished a dime out of what little change I had left and dialed a Sausalito number. Someone answered the telephone.

"Buenas noches," I said. "This is the international operator calling from Tijuana, Mexico. Will you accept a collect call from the Tijuana city jail from a Senor Jose Goodey?"

"Joe!" said Rachel Schute. "That was a pretty short trip to Mexico, wasn't it? Or are you really in Tijuana?"

"Not really."

"And you're not in jail?"

"Not just now," I said truthfully. "I was giving some thought to coming over to see you in a little while."

"I'd like that," she said. "I've got a houseful of dinner guests, but they won't be here forever."

"Anybody I know?"

"Everybody," she said. "But nobody you'd care to talk to."

"I'm an antisocial bastard."

"You are," she agreed. "Do you think you'll be here in about an hour?"

"That depends on a couple of things," I said, "but I'll try. If you haven't gotten rid of those bums by then, I'll throw them off the sun deck." I'm a tough guy.

"See you, Joe," she said.

The taxi dropped me at the corner of my street. As I was walking toward Lum Kee's, I was pleased to see my car still standing there. With my luck it could have been towed away. My suitcases were still in the trunk, and there didn't seem to be any particular reason for going up to the apartment. It was highly likely that Maher or one of his pals was still somewhere around, although there was no squad car on the block.

As I was passing Lum Kee's shop on the other side of the street, the shop door opened and Lum Kee came out backward, looking like an overweight beetle in his black coat

"Hello, Lum!" I said, just for the hell of it.

You'd have thought I'd touched him with a high-tension wire. Lum started, jumped back about a foot, and looked as though he was going to run back through the closed door.

Instead, he turned around with the awkward speed of a

man who didn't want to see something but knew he had to get it over with. "Joe Goodey?" he said. "Can it be you?"

"Sure it can," I said. "The police decided that they didn't want me after all."

"What?" he said, and I could tell that he didn't have any idea what I was talking about. He was still staring at me as if he couldn't believe what he saw before him. "But the boy said—" he started. Then he stopped, clamped his mouth shut, and just stared some more.

"I'm glad to see that you're so touched to have me back," I said. "I never suspected that you cared."

"Sure, sure," Lum Kee muttered in a distracted way. "I've got to go now. I must go." He shuffled toward the corner at high speed.

Shrugging, I continued on to my car. I checked the trunk, and my suitcases looked untouched. There was no reason to go upstairs at all.

I started driving toward Sausalito. It was only a twenty-five minute drive, even on a busy Friday night, so I had a bit of time to spare. For thinking. When I got to the Marin County end of the Golden Gate Bridge, it was still only ten minutes to eleven. I didn't want to get in on the tail end of Rachel's dinner party, so I cut into the lane leading to the observation area at the end of the bridge.

The night was too hazy to let viewers get much out of the San Francisco skyline, but a parking place was hard to find. As a semipro voyeur, I canvassed the parked cars I passed and was surprised to find so many contained only one person. Maybe a lot of other people had things to think out.

I found a slot between an MGB and a big Buick convertible. Outside, Led Zeppelin and Mozart bumped heads, and I settled down for a few minutes of concentrated thought. It's times like that when a detective ought to smoke. A cigarette somehow lends credibility to heavy thinking. A man slowly destroying his lungs is hardly open to charges of daydreaming. But I didn't even have a stick of gum.

What I had was a murder—or maybe two, if I took a professional interest in Chub's death—to solve. But first, Tina D'Oro. Who had something to gain from Tina's death? Or, on the other hand, who disliked her enough to kill her whether there was anything to gain from it or not?

I didn't yet know all the players in the final drama of Tina D'Oro, but any way I looked at it, Mayor Sanford F. Kolchik looked like the odds-on favorite. Who was involved romantically with Tina? S.F.K. Who stood to lose a great deal if that involvement became known? S.F.K. Who was the most likely target for blackmail if that was Tina's game? Three out of three.

Kolchik had a whole lot of other credentials which qualified him to be my man. Not the least of which was a hard, ruthless brother whose career was as firmly attached to Sandy Kolchik's as the earth is to the sun. If Sandy took a fall, The Brother was a goner. Perhaps outweighing all this was the fact that Kolchik was the one potential suspect that Johnny Maher wouldn't touch. He was virgin territory, and he was all mine. I had the additional satisfaction of knowing that if Sandy was had for Tina's murder, he couldn't very well get tough with me over his cousin. Or could he? It was worth thinking about.

But not just then. A Sheriff's Department prowl car had pulled into the parking area and was making the circuit with his spotlight. It was probably just some young punk deputy getting revenge on the parkers for having a better time than he was, but I wasn't in the mood to find out. There's something about being a recent ex-cop which encourages paranoia. Mine didn't need much encouragement. I rapidly started the Morris and got out of there, which was probably what the Sheriff's boy wanted in the first place.

Sausalito was a small fishing village. About fifty years ago. But now it was a strange mélange of the idle rich, hustling merchants, and descendants of the original fishermen, who hated, scorned, and envied the first two categories. Rachel Schute fell into the first class and lived in a cantilevered, multi-decked phantasmagoria high up over the waterfront, with the San Francisco skyline as its private light show.

Rachel was saying goodbye to the last of her departing guests as I pulled into the shallow parking area under the lower deck. I recognized Moses Stanfield's showy, green Continental. Ho-hum, I thought, it's old home night. The Stanfields were being shepherded down the steep wooden steps as I came up them with a suitcase in my hand. I could have been the Fuller brush man on a night call.

"Oh, hello, Joe," Rachel said easily. "You're just in time to meet Justice and Mrs. Stanfield."

"A pleasure, Justice," I said, giving him the old fraternity grip and a winning smile. "Mrs. Stanfield and I are old friends." I slipped her a half wink. "Not leaving so soon, I hope?" Like hell I did.

Mrs. Stanfield had had just enough to drink to be caught midway between ladylike gaiety and slatternly sullenness. A drink sooner, and she'd have greeted me like an old shipmate. A drink later, and she'd have bitten my head off and spat it in my face. As it was, she paused, one foot in the air, and looked at me as a poker player would at a hand containing two jacks of diamonds. She didn't miss the suitcase, either.

The justice obviously didn't remember my name. "A pleasure," he lied absent-mindedly. "We really must be going, Rachel. Lovely dinner." And they were gone. The big Lincoln sucked a couple gallons of gas into its carburetors and ate up several hundred yards of street. We were alone.

"Evening," I said to Rachel. "Are there any leftovers? I

didn't have any real dinner. Let's go into the kitchen, and I'll tell you where I didn't eat it."

Rachel stood poised on the top step. She was smiling, but as usual she looked as though she couldn't decide whether to fall into my arms or kick me into the street. It may sound fishy for me to keep insisting on it, but Rachel Schute was a hell of a good-looking woman. Especially all kitted out in a jade-colored dress that cost more than I ever made in a month and with that pale strawberry hair pushed up over her pointy ears like small ostrich plumes. Rachel's pale-blue eyes were a bit naked and raw-looking, the way redheads' often are, but she knew how to get the best out of them with make-up. At three in the morning, with a face full of tears and a mouth full of recriminations, she was dead ugly, but right now she'd do just fine.

"Sure, Joe," she said, weakening as usual. "Let's go see what's left." She held out a warm, freckled left hand to me, and I took it. The strength of the squeeze she gave my hand told me she hadn't quite given up on me. She should have known better. Hell, I should have known better and married her. But neither of us did.

Rachel's spade housemaid-cook shot me her usual I-know-you-hustler look, adding, "Good night, Mrs. Schute," before leaving us really alone. I sat down at the kitchen table and started ravaging what was left of the prime rib and potatoes julienne, while Rachel perched herself across the table and waited for me to bring her up to date.

I didn't disappoint her. I told her most of what I knew, leaving out only the mayor's involvement and Tina's diary. I could tell from the way she was listening that she didn't neces-sarily believe that the department brought me back—me, whom they'd just thrown out—just to look into the murder of a go-go girl, even Tina. So she didn't have to believe me.

I finished off the prime rib and about a pint of chocolate-rum ice cream. Then I put my hand on hers across the table.

"Come on," I said, partly because I knew it was expected of me, "let's go to bed."

"Sometimes, Joe," Rachel said, "I think you're just using me." But the way she turned her hand to meet mine said this wasn't yet a Federal offense.

"Could be," I said, tugging her to her feet.

11

IT WAS IN THE MORNING THAT I ALWAYS WISHED I COULD bring myself to marry the Widow Schute. We were sitting on the top deck, blinking in the soft-lemon sunshine, with Sausalito and the bay laid out for us to spit on if we felt like it. Miss Black Power was back dishing out the scrambled eggs, bacon, croissants, and fresh grapefruit juice. I could tell she didn't like me because she always put my eggs off-center on the plate.

Rachel was sitting there in a hundred-and-fifty-dollar dressing gown, looking well-laid and altogether too content with life to bother settling the guerrilla warfare going on at the end of the table between Ramsey and Donald, the two older boys. And Joey, the baby, was busy mashing his scrambled eggs into his highchair tray. He'd not yet been born when his father, the late, rich Howard Schute had driven his car off a seventy-five-foot cliff above Stinson Beach. I hadn't known Howard Schute, but he couldn't have been too bad if Rachel liked him.

My friend, the maid, brought me the *Chronicle* as if she were giving up one of her kidneys, and it didn't take me long to find the report of Chub's untimely end. Not that it carried screaming headlines. The story was all but buried on the back page next to a laxative ad and simply said that a Mr. Seymour F.—for what? I wondered—Kroll of New York City had been found in a North Beach apartment house dead of stab wounds. The police were pursuing their investigations. A one-day non-sensation. I wondered if there was somebody in New York who would care.

On the front page, the *Chronicle* was still pumping Tina's death for what it was worth and quoting Johnny Maher's noncommittal statements about the likelihood of the killer being caught, tried, and executed in time for Sunday brunch. There was a good deal of lip-licking over preparations for the memorial service at midday at St. Timothy's, the hippest church in North Beach. It promised to be a four-star occasion. It was bound to be open-coffin, but would Tina be topless?

Breakfast can't last forever, and I had a visit to pay across the way on Belvedere Island. If I turned slightly to the left, I could see Belvedere, but couldn't pick out the house.

The boys kicked up such a fuss when I said I had to leave that Rachel didn't have a chance really to get started. Not that she was much of a fuss maker. She could say things with her eyes and a slight lift of her upper lip that you couldn't get across with forty-five minutes of shouting. I kissed her warmly but noncommittally, wrestled with the boys all the way down the three flights of outside steps, and waved like hell until my car was out of sight. There was a damned fine family for somebody who wanted a family.

It was a pleasant, sunny ride from Sausalito to Belvedere, right around the blunt blade of bay which splits that end of Marin County. When I passed through Mill Valley I gave a thought to Ralph Lehman up there on his little hill, trying to hold everything together for another nine months so that he could retire. He'd be lucky.

Belvedere's not really an island, but it likes to think it is. Since most of the houses on Belvedere have their backs rudely turned to the narrow road that spirals around it, the casual rubbernecker wouldn't know how really luxurious the houses are.

About two thirds of the way up, I pulled off the road into a little carport in front of a three-car redwood garage. Even the garage had a good view over Tiburon toward the Richmond-San Rafael Bridge. I was just putting a foot on the carefully graveled ground when a voice said, "What do you want here, Goodey?"

I couldn't see who it belonged to, but I knew the voice. It was Stoney Karras, Sgt. Stoney Karras, late of the Docks Squad, now detached for rather special duty. I hate talking to people I can't see, so I waited until he appeared from behind a thick, stunted cypress tree next to the garage. Karras didn't look like much in a cheap Robert Hall special the color of grape pulp and ancient oxblood loafers, but I respected him as a hard man in a hard job.

"I want to see the man, Stoney."

"What if he don't want to see you?"

"Try him and see," I suggested.

Stoney shrugged and went over me with his fat fingers like an amateur pianist. He didn't find anything because my police special was still in the suitcase. Then he told me not to bother wandering around while he checked out my popularity rating with the squire. I could have told him the answer to that one, but I didn't think Kolchik would refuse to see me. He was too interested in the job I was supposed to do to play it that cool.

"Okay, come on," said Stoney when he reappeared from the house, but I could tell from his expression that he thought the mayor was making a mistake. Stoney would have had me thrown into the bay. That's why Stoney wasn't the mayor. Maybe he should have been.

Stoney herded me out onto a brick terrace at the front of the house, grunted something, and left me standing there. I was alone. A couple of leather-strapped sun loungers pointed out to sea, and a low, driftwood table held a big, kidney-shaped ceramic ashtray and a Mexican silver cigarette box. On the silver box was a small brass bell.

Somebody cleared his throat theatrically behind me. I turned around to see Mayor Kolchik coming out of the dark recesses of the house.

Kolchik was a short, dark man with a potato nose and the physical stature of a natural clown. But there was nothing clownish about his black, deep-set eyes. They told you that everything you assumed about him at first glance was a mistake, and you'd better know it. They meant business. His outfit was sporty—a three-quarter-sleeved mustard shirt, Balboa-blue slacks with a razor crease, and open-weave sandals. But his heart wasn't in it. He could have really relaxed in a midnight-blue pinstripe with one-inch cuffs.

Neither of us knew exactly how to start. We knew too much about each other to be strangers. He knew I'd shot his cousin, and I knew about Tina. We couldn't start with a businesslike handshake.

"You're Goodey," he said.

I wanted to say, "You're Kolchik," but chickened out and just nodded.

"You wanted to see me?" he said.

"Yes, I wanted to talk to you about Tina D'Oro," I said, feeling a bit silly and exposed.

Kolchik looked as though someone had given him a tough riddle, and he was working on it. Apparently he hadn't expected such a call on this sunny Saturday morning. He peered at me as if I were a junior accountant who'd lost a decimal point. He frowned.

"Does my brother know you're over here?"

"He told me to investigate Tina's murder," I said, "but he didn't tell me how. I'm one of those self-starters you hear about."

He didn't like that. It came too close to wise-guyism to suit him, and he frowned again. He was a good frowner.

"So I'm your number-one suspect, eh?" he said. That brought out a small, wrinkled smile, and I began to like him a little. But only a little.

"If you weren't a possible suspect," I said, "you wouldn't have wanted to try to find out who killed Tina and eliminate you as a suspect. When Lehman told me just how it was, I volunteered to come back."

"You wanted to help me," he said.

"I wanted to help myself. The way Lehman told it, unless I came back willingly and tried to bail you out, you and The Brother were going to get nasty about me shooting your cousin."

"If that's what Lehman said, there must be some truth in it," Kolchik said. He smiled again. "So that's what they call Bruno, eh? The Brother."

"That's what I call him. I've heard him called worse."

"A lot of people have the wrong slant on Bruno," he said. "He's a bit rough, perhaps, but he's got one great quality that makes up for everything. He's loyal."

"Loyal to what?"

"To me, Goodey. To me," Kolchik said complacently. "What are you loyal to?"

Before I could answer, he moved over to the driftwood table and took up the small bell. He gave it a few brisk shakes, and almost immediately a short, ugly girl with a Little Nemo haircut came out onto the terrace with an expectant look on her face. She was wearing a mauve slack suit with a small apron which seemed to turn it into a uniform. She ignored me and turned her face to Kolchik as if he were the sun.

"Let's have a drink, Goodey," he said. "I make some very good beer. Irina, will you please bring us a bottle of the home-made beer from the cellar?"

She moved back into the house with a slightly pigeon-toed walk, and Kolchik gestured toward the deck chairs. "Let's sit down and enjoy the sun," he said. "It's one of God's great gifts. Now, you were about to tell me what you're loyal to. Or maybe to whom." The "to whom" came right out of Business English 1 A (night school division), but he got it out without falling flat on his face.

I didn't have to think very hard. "To me," I said.

I could see that he thought this was a bit crass. It offended his Polish-American sense of respect for family, nation, and institutions.

"Not to the police force?" he asked with raised eyebrows. He meant, "Not to me?"

"I'm not on the police force anymore," I said. "You had me kicked off."

"Oh, yes," he said, shrugging as if he'd forgotten to pay the milkman or some other small oversight. "But you'll be back on the police force, won't you, after you clear up this...other matter?"

"I don't know," I said. "But about this *other matter—*"

But he wasn't listening. He was looking past me at the sliding door into the house, and I turned to follow his eyes. Coming onto the terrace was a woman in a shiny, chromium-plated wheelchair which she was propelling with thin, muscular arms. On a tray over her lap was a pitcher of beer with a thick head of foam and two tall pilsner glasses. She maneuvered the wheelchair with the expertise of long practice.

Everything about the woman was gray, and she fought the somber shade by wearing a vividly flowered red dress and a shocking shade of carmine lipstick. Her tapered nails were drops of fresh blood. But behind this show of color, she was like a vampire's victim, drained of all but the dregs of life and fighting every inch of the way. Behind her dull silver skin, veins like very minor roads on a map seemed to be fading out before my eyes.

Kolchik was up from the sun lounger and behind her chair with the agility of a man half his age. Reluctantly she stopped propelling the chair and allowed herself to be pushed.

"This is my wife," Kolchik said proudly, wheeling her between our two loungers. "Dear, this is Joe Goodey. He's a detective looking into the murder of Tina D'Oro."

I jumped up feeling faintly guilty. "I could come back at a more convenient time," I said, "if—"

"No, Mr. Goodey," she said, giving me a cold, dry hand, "there won't be a more convenient time. This is fine." She paused briefly. "Aren't you the detective who shot Sanford's cousin? What extremely bad luck!"

I didn't know if she meant that I or old Stanislaus had had the bad luck, but I nodded. "Yes, I'm afraid I'm the one."

"Have you been to see him at the hospital yet?"

"No," I said. "Things have been a little hectic since then, and I haven't had a chance. I don't think I'd be very welcome anyway."

"Of course you would," she said sternly, looking up at my face with once-indigo eyes glazed with a gray sheen. "Cousin Stanislaus will be wondering what sort of man shot him."

"I'll try to get to see him soon," I promised.

The mayor had poured out two perfect glasses of beer and

was holding one out toward me. "Drink this," he said, "and you'll never drink commercial beer again. It's a recipe my grandfather stole from the bishop of Cracow."

It just tasted like beer to me, but I tried to look like a man drinking the best beer he'd ever experienced. I don't think I succeeded, but Kolchik swallowed his disappointment and the rest of his glass of beer and immediately poured himself another. Not to be outdone, I chug-a-lugged the rest of mine and held out my glass. Hizzoner brightened considerably, and I could tell that we were well on the way to being best buddies.

But how do you raise such a delicate matter as the late Tina D'Oro with even a best buddy with his crippled wife sitting there admiring his bobbing Adam's apple as he drank beer?

"Mayor," I said, "the matter I came to see you about is a rather delicate one. I think we'd better talk privately."

"That won't be necessary, Goodey," he answered, wiping his mouth with the back of his hand and missing a bit of foam. "Mrs. Kolchik knew all about Tina. I have no secrets from her. So go right ahead."

I still hesitated. I'm as modern and sophisticated as the next man, but I'm still young enough to think that there's something unwholesome about swinging geriatric cases. But then, maybe Kolchik didn't see himself that way.

"That's right, Officer," said Mrs. Kolchik, smiling up at me. "I knew about Tina. You see, it's been many years since my health has been good enough to allow me to be a complete wife to Sanford." She didn't have to hit me over the head with a bread board. I knew what she was getting at. "And," she went on, "Sanford is still a youthful and vigorous man. So we decided years ago that it would be best if he were free to seek the company of younger, stronger women. It was my idea. You see, Mr. Goodey, I am a European woman, really. I hope I am not embarrassing you."

"Oh, no," I lied. I'd really have preferred not to be let in on the family secrets, but it looked as if I already was. "But I hope you'll excuse me if I'm just as frank."

"Of course," they said together, all smiles.

"Well, then, Mayor," I said, "with the number of girls in San Francisco available to a man in your position, how could you have been stupid enough to choose one like Tina in a situation as public, if not more public, than your own?"

I thought that would shake him up. But he didn't seem to mind a bit, just smiled boyishly, looked fondly at Mrs. K., and said: "Tina reminded me of Maria when she was younger."

Christ, another complication. Who's this Maria, and how does she fit in? Then it came to me: Maria was Mrs. Kolchik. I don't know why it occurred to me, other than the expression on Kolchik's face. She looked about as much like Tina as I did. Trying not to be too obvious, I searched Mrs. K.'s ravaged face and body for any faint resemblance to Tina's plastic lushness. I suppose my face showed it.

"I was not always a cripple, Mr. Goodey," Mrs. Kolchik said softly, and I felt ashamed of myself. "However, I must say that I never looked anything like Tina D'Oro. I fear it was just Sanford's imagination. But I found it flattering, I admit."

"You were far more beautiful than Tina, Maria," said Kolchik with a great deal of enthusiasm. But then he remembered that he was talking of a girl who had only recently and violently died, and he crossed himself.

"You were asking questions, Goodey," he said, bringing things back into official tracks. "What else do you want to know?"

"When did you last see Tina?" I asked.

"Tuesday afternoon," he said quickly, "between two thirty-five and four o'clock."

"Did you notice anything unusual about her? Did she seem

depressed or worried about anything? Would she have told you if she had been?"

"No, to the first two questions," he said. "And I doubt it very much, to the third. Tina didn't seem any different than usual."

"And how was that?" I wondered how a bimbo like Tina appeared to a big man like Kolchik.

"Simple, happy, uncomplicated, uncomplaining," he said. "A very relaxing girl to be with. Of course, she was vain, obsessed with herself, her body, her career. Tina had the idea that wiggling about to loud music was some kind of art form. No, more than that—a power for positive good in the world. I believe she thought she was making a personal contribution to world peace and general enlightenment."

"Did Tina tell you much about herself?" I asked. "About her past, I mean—where she came from, what she did before she became a big topless star."

He shook his head. "No, I asked her to tell me about her life, but she was always very vague. She didn't want to talk about that. She did say once that she came from someplace over in the East Bay, but that's all. Tina wasn't interested in the past. The past was dead and buried as far as she was concerned. She knew only one direction—ahead. Upward and onward, that was Tina, and she was in a terrible hurry to get there."

"To get where?" I asked.

"To the top," Kolchik said. "The movies, Las Vegas, Broadway. You name it, Tina was going to get there and be bigger and better than any of them. The Jungle was just a phase. She had her foot out for the next rung on the ladder, but I don't think she knew where or what it was. But she knew the direction she was going."

"Mr. Kolchik," I said, "did you know before Tina was killed that she kept a diary and that you were in it?"

"No," he said, "I had no idea. I do know that she seemed to understand the need for discretion, that it couldn't be publicly known that we were—friends. I never asked her if she was writing anything down."

I had more questions I didn't like to raise with my new buddy, Sandy, but I had to.

"Mayor," I said, "was Tina or anybody else blackmailing you about your relationship with her?"

"No!" he said positively. "Nobody."

"Do you know if she told anybody about you and her? Anybody at all?"

He thought deeply for a few moments. "She could have," he said, "but I don't know that she did. It may sound odd, but I didn't know Tina very well. I don't even know who her friends were or if she had any. Ours was a very—limited friendship, you see."

I did see, if he was telling the truth. I plunged on. "And your— friendship, Mayor," I asked, "how had it been going lately? Had you had any arguments, fights, disagreements of any kind?"

He seemed honestly puzzled. "No," he said, "nothing like that. It really wasn't that sort of relationship."

"Well, was the nature of your relationship changing or on the verge of changing? I mean, if I'm not being too personal, were you tired of her? Did her attitude toward you seem any different? Or were things just going along smoothly?"

"To tell the truth, Goodey," he said, "I was giving some thought to—to seeing Tina less often. After all, with the election coming up—" The rest of the sentence faded in the fresh morning air.

"Did Tina know that? Did she object?"

"She didn't even know, Goodey," he said. "I hardly knew it myself. I hadn't really made up my mind yet."

If Kolchik was the guilty party, he was going to be a hard man to trap. He seemed too damned honest. "One last question, Mayor," I said, getting up from the sun lounger. "Can you prove where you were at the time Tina was murdered?"

"No," he said. "At about three in the morning on Thursday I was asleep here—alone."

"We have separate bedrooms, Mr. Goodey," said Mrs. Kolchik, who had been listening closely to our exchange.

"So," said the mayor, "you can see that I have no ironclad alibi. You'll just have to go on suspecting me."

"I'll do that," I said and began to make well-I'm-leaving noises. The late-morning sun beating down on this terrace was very pleasant, but it wasn't getting me any closer to where I wanted to be. Mrs. K. said good-by with a ruined smile, and the mayor walked me to the door, where Stoney Karras waited with a face like a garbage man making a pickup. Kolchik waved him away and offered me the big hand he'd forgotten when I'd arrived.

"Good-by," he said. "I hope you're successful in your search —and soon."

"Me too," I said, taking back my hand and turning to walk back to my car.

"Goodey," he said, and I stopped and turned back toward him, "do you really think it's possible that I killed Tina?"

"It's possible," I said. No use letting him get complacent. "I haven't heard anything yet which rules it out."

"Good," he said to my surprise. "You keep on suspecting everybody, and you'll end up getting the right person. Maybe you're a better detective than we all thought."

"Maybe." I turned again to go.

"Goodey," he said.

This was getting monotonous. I was beginning to feel like

one of those little shooting-gallery rabbits that turns sharply at the end of each row and repeats his path.

"Yeah?"

"Don't waste any time."

I answered that one with a meaningless look and walked through the doorway to the back of the house. Stoney was waiting for me. He didn't look friendly.

"I'll see you off," he said.

"Don't strain yourself."

"It's no strain. It's a pleasure."

As I got in my car, Stoney said, "I don't like ex-cops."

I backed up and got the right slant to the road before I answered. "Neither do I," I said, driving close enough to make him back up against the white-painted wall. That wouldn't do his suit any good. In the mirror he didn't look happy.

12

Sᴛ. Tɪᴍᴏᴛʜʏ's ᴡᴀs ᴀ ᴛᴀʟʟ, ᴄʀᴏᴏᴋᴇᴅ, ʜɪᴘ ʟɪᴛᴛʟᴇ ᴄʜᴜʀᴄʜ in the shadow of Coit Tower. It was the kind of church that held rock masses and nudist baptisms. The curate was a weedy little West Point dropout who was on record calling Cardinal McGinty a "tired, old, worn-out, neo-Fascist prick." It was that kind of church, and the waiting list to get married there was as long as a bookie's memory.

It was still half an hour before Tina's memorial service, but the block in front of St. Timothy's looked like the closing scene of *Day of the Locust*. You couldn't have cast that crowd at Twentieth Century Fox. You name it: hippies, Chinese pimps, spade socialites, the dregs of Nob Hill's rearguard bacchants, the Broadway cognoscenti—they were all there, milling around for the benefit of the television cameras and the nine o'clock news. The tall, oak double doors of St Timothy's were still closed.

From their windows the natives looked down on the throngers in third-generation Italian wonder and occasionally threw down something that wasn't too heavy or too valuable.

An old buddy of mine, Sgt. Jack Sweet, the uncrowned king of North Beach, was jostling about in the crowd, using a bit of muscle on the more obvious pickpockets, rubbing up against the prettier girls, trying to nip mayhem in the bud, and enjoying every minute of it. Better him than me.

I stashed my car safely around the corner and edged up to the mob gingerly. If Tina's murderer had been standing in the middle of that crowd with a confession pinned to his chest, I don't think I'd have gone in after him. Somebody tapped me on the shoulder in an authoritative manner. He didn't quite knock me down.

Rather than risk another attack, I turned around and found Bert Coney, newspaper columnist, celebrity maker, and claimant to the title of "Mr. San Francisco." He was looking at me as if he owned me and the square mile I was standing on.

"You're Joe Goodey," he told me in a way that made me want to believe him. Coney carried his round little head at about fifteen degrees off vertical, and his very expensive toupee seemed to be holding on for dear life. He had weary little eyes, resting comfortably in nests of wrinkles, and a face that had been introduced to many an expensive bottle of wine.

I didn't deny the accusation, so he went on: "You knew Tina, didn't you? Maybe you've got an angle for my column tomorrow. They're crying for my copy down at the office, and all I can get from this crowd of scum is 'so young, so beautiful' crap. I can't use that."

"I didn't know her all that well," I said, still casing the crowd over the top of his head.

"Then what are you doing here?" he asked. "Kolchik didn't take you back on the force, did he?" An idea seemed to glow at the back of his dull eyes. "Say, you didn't lay her, did you? I wonder how many guys here today laid Tina D'Oro? That's an angle."

I didn't argue with him. "No, I didn't lay her," I said, "but it might not be too late. I understand it's going to be open coffin." That took even Coney by surprise. He stopped searching the mob for Tina's ex-lovers and looked at me with new interest.

"Now, that," he said, "is really sick." He wasn't being critical, just remarking on a new discovery, like peanut-butter yogurt. "You cops are a hard lot. Tina's body is hardly cold yet, and..."

"Yeah," I said, "so young, so beautiful. You'll have to excuse me now." I pushed past him with my eyes on the horizon as if I were searching for someone, but I just wanted to get away from him and away from that crowd.

HOLY MARTYRS CEMETERY WAS A LITTLE PATCH OF WASTE ground on the wrong side of Millbrae. Unlike St. Timothy's, it wasn't fashionable. Nobody who was anybody would be caught there dead or alive. But that was where they were going to bury Tina. And I couldn't find it.

It was an uneventful drive down the Bayshore past the airport. I turned at Millbrae Avenue and pulled off the road at a place called Bruce's Eatery. I asked a scared-looking little man behind the counter if he knew the way to Holy Martyrs Cemetery.

He couldn't have been all that scared. I could have crushed him with my thumb, but he answered, "Did you come in here for something to eat or just ask directions?"

"Does it make a difference?"

"Yes. If you're not going to order anything, I can't remember where Holy Martyrs is. There's something about a cash-register bell that stirs my memory. Without it, I'm a case of walking amnesia."

"How big a tab does a guy have to run up to get a straight answer?" I asked, settling onto a counter stool. "I don't think I can afford total recall."

"Try a cheeseburger, French fries, and coffee," he said, peeling the paper separator off a square of frozen something and dropping it on the grease-blackened griddle. "It's cheaper than wasting gasoline in this end of nowhere."

That cheeseburger worked miracles. It tasted pretty good, and it jogged his memory to a rosy glow.

The gates to the cemetery were ancient with rust, and the old man who said he was the caretaker refused to open them until the funeral party arrived. There was no use in doing the same job twice, he said, leaning on a rake I knew damned well he never used. I could have bribed my way in, but I figured I might as well wait there, admiring the veins in his nose, as sit next to a freshly dug grave.

We didn't have much to say to each other, so he just leaned and I just sat while the flies buzzed around us and more dust settled on my Morris. We'd probably be there frozen like a cheap tableau to this day if a beautiful black Cadillac hearse hadn't swept into the cemetery's short, rubble-strewn drive and come to rest about an inch from my back bumper. A pebble-grained chauffeur in wraparound sun glasses frowned through his tinted wind screen at the back of my head. The top of the hearse was festooned with sprays and horseshoes of brilliant hothouse flowers, looking waxy enough to melt in the hot sun.

Behind the hearse came another black Caddy and behind that a blue-white Rolls Royce Silver Shadow which shimmered in the heat like something out of Fellini.

That was it—the whole funeral cortege. But it was enough for the old caretaker to creak into action with a big ring of keys. Eventually he got the right one into the keyhole, but then couldn't get the gate to swing open. I got out and pushed as he pulled, but we still couldn't do it. I looked over my shoulder at the hearse driver. He couldn't see me until his partner in the front seat, a smooth character who looked like a beauty queen's favorite uncle, turned to him and said something short and sharp.

The chauffeur came out, clapped his fawn gloves together with impatient energy, and put his weight onto the gate like the Detroit Lions' front four. It screeched open with an Inner Sanctum note. With a see-you-sissy look at me, the driver headed back for his hearse. I was glad to see that his pretty gloves and uniform shoulder were stained with rust.

The caretaker waved me vaguely off to the left on a weed-overgrown track. It didn't take me long to spot the big pile of earth that had been moved to make room for Tina. I drove past at a discreet distance to leave space for the funeral procession. By the time I'd parked and had walked back, the hearse had stopped, and the driver and his boss were rolling Tina's coffin down a little portable ramp.

The casket was draped with what looked like a million white gardenias sewn together into a blanket. The edges of the flowers scraped along the brown earth, leaving a little trail of petals to the edge of the freshly dug grave. The chauffeur then got busy untying the rest of the floral tributes from the top of the hearse.

Meanwhile, a door of the elongated Cadillac sedan had been eased open silently. Another chauffeur and a tall old gentleman in a tail coat were assisting a woman dressed entirely in black from the back seat. Her face was completely obscured by an opaque black veil, but from the size of her and a flash of a muscular calf, it looked to me as if she could have carried both of them and the casket. But just then she was blubbering too loudly and vividly to pull her own weight, so the old boy and his driver were edging her in the same direction as the casket.

The Rolls Royce had stopped too, and a back door was open. But nobody was getting out. I recognized the driver as one of the monkeys Fat Phil let hang around The Jungle. He was sitting behind the wheel, reading a magazine, with one foot cocked up on a window ledge. It was obvious that he was no mourner, just an honest citizen earning a buck.

I walked over to the open door of the Rolls and peered in.

Sitting square in the middle of the big back seat was Fat Phil, and it looked as though he needed a half-size bigger car. Despite the arctic blast of the air conditioner, sweat was rolling out of his low hairline, and he was moaning softly like a half-crushed puppy.

"Goodey," he said when he could gather the strength, "I can't make it. I thought I could, but I can't." He took a gasping breath. "And after I rented this car too. The best they had. Costing me a fortune."

"It's a business expense, Phil," I said consolingly. "You can write it off. That is, if you live."

"If I live," he echoed. "I don't know. Hey, did you see the blanket of gardenias? Great, hey? It set me back a packet, but nothing's too good for Tina."

I was going to tell him to take it out of Tina's side of the profits, but then I felt someone tugging genteelly at my sleeve. It was the second chauffeur, an aging black with an old razor scar running down through one nostril.

"Sir," he said without conscious irony, "the service is about to begin if you would like to join us."

I thought about trying to help Fat Phil out of the Rolls, but he'd closed his eyes again and had gone back to breathing through his mouth. Turning with the chauffeur, I caught the scene at graveside. The big woman in black had been handed over to the younger undertaker and was rearing and bucking at the edge of the grave. It was all he and the other driver could do to keep her from toppling in after the casket. At the head of the open grave, the old gentleman with the white hair had a large book open, which I took for a Bible, and was looking up over it at me with disapproval. He also sneaked a look at a watch peeping out from his faultless white shirt cuff.

"No priest?" I asked my guide.

"Father Shearer," he said through motionless lips, "wasn't able to make it. In the commotion after the church service he was nicked by the fuzz. Mr. McDavitt will do the reading." If he learned that style of talking any place but San Quentin, I'd misjudged my man.

Just as I was taking my place across the grave from the bereaved lady and her two anchors, a voice cried out: "Hold it!" A San Francisco taxi had come to a stop behind the Rolls, and four men came piling out. I recognized two of them as reporters. The other two had bulky press cameras.

McDavitt looked even more pissed off. One of the photographers ran around to the head of the grave and began badgering him to raise the casket again so that he could get a picture of it going down. McDavitt refused, copping another peek at his watch, and tried to calm everybody for the service, which, unless I was wrong, was going to be short and sweet. The photographer settled for a high-angle picture of the casket in the grave, and the two reporters stationed themselves on either side of the lady mourner, ready to pounce as soon as the first shovel of earth hit the casket. The other photographer had fallen back for some long shots of this splendid little scene and was now zeroing in on Fat Phil's rented Rolls for a bit of color.

Old McDavitt got his pretty white teeth into a text which began: "We gather today to say farewell to this child. For child she was, as are we all in the eyes of God..." It wasn't a bad start, but I couldn't hear any of the rest of it for the wailing that commenced from the old party across the grave.

Undeterred, McDavitt plowed on with the text, mouthing the words as eloquently as if he were burying a queen. When he closed the big book there were tears in his watery blue eyes. He dropped a signal, and the black driver lofted a big spadeful of dirt down into the grave.

The dirt hit the box with a muffled thud.

With that sound the wailing and moaning across the way suddenly stopped. A dusty silence fell over our little funeral party, and even the photographers stopped snapping for a moment. Then the lone mourner raised two muscular arms tipped with black gauntlets and lifted her veils revealing thick coils of copper-wire hair and a face like a retired fullback.

She couldn't have been less than sixty years old, and every one of those years had been a hard one, judging by the souvenirs they'd left on her old mug. One incisor was missing, and she had three chins making inverted stairsteps down to the high ruching at the neck of her black dress.

Her complexion was that of an old wineskin that had been dipped in the flour barrel, and her eyes were hollow and cried out. The two reporters converged on her like freeloaders after the last cocktail sausage.

"Mrs. Barton," said the big one, an ex-police reporter named Royster I'd often seen sleeping on a sofa at police head-quarters, "would you..."

The little one, a lad who looked like a new cub on a high-school paper, tried to sneak under Royster's arm and get at the old woman. "I'm from the *Examiner*, Mrs. Barton," he said, "and I wonder if..."

The woman wheeled on them like a battered old lioness, worn out but still dangerous.

"Piss off the both of you," she snarled. "I've got nothing to say to the press. All you did when my poor girl was alive was hound her and write lies about her. Leave me alone."

This set the kid from the *Examiner* back on his heels, but Royster had badgered too many bereaved survivors in his day to let her off that easily. "Hell, Maggie," he insisted, "all I want—"

My eye was caught by something big and white going away. It was Fat Phil in his rented Rolls. I looked to see if he had taken back his blanket of gardenias, but it was still at graveside. I suppose there's not much of a market for used gardenia blankets.

The drivers were putting away their equipment while the two undertakers were standing discreetly at a distance, waiting to get a word in with Mrs. Barton. Maybe they wanted to hand her the bill. I couldn't wait to witness that encounter.

But then I saw something else more interesting. Far across the cemetery, trying to look invisible in the shelter of one of the few large monuments, was yet another funeral guest. But one too shy to mix it up at graveside. It occurred to me that it might be worthwhile to interview this retiring mourner. But at that moment he spotted me spotting him and started making toward a late-model sedan parked near the cemetery gate.

I'm no speed merchant, but he must have been way out of training. I beat him by several dozen noses and was leaning against the car door when he came puffing up. He was a little guy in a dapper tan summer suit and dusty perforated brown shoes. He couldn't have been much over thirty, but his indeterminate brown hair was withering on top like last summer's rutabaga patch, and he'd soon be bald. His pale, shoe-shaped face was pleasant, but just then it wasn't helped much by the streams of tears running from his red-rimmed eyes. He was obviously suffering, and I felt like a heel bothering him. But I did anyway.

"Excuse me," I said, flashing my private buzzer quickly. "I'm a detective. Did you know Tina D'Oro?"

That must have been exactly the wrong question. It

doubled him over with sobbing and had him clawing for a big, white handkerchief from an inside pocket. The monogram was "F.I." That rang a bell from Tina's diary.

"I can't talk to you now," he gasped through the hanky. His free hand dipped into a coat pocket and shoved a small, white card at me. "Please, please," he said, "come see me this evening. The address...the address..."

He broke down again, and I got out of his way fast. I can't take too much crying. If he was faking it, he deserved an Oscar, and would be too clever for me to handle anyway. He grabbed blindly for the car-door handle, stumbled behind the wheel, and the car lurched through the gates and disappeared.

Now that the danger of being run down by suicidal mourners had lessened considerably, I took a look at the card he'd given me. "Fletcher Irving, M.D.," it said in fine capitals. The address was out on Ocean Avenue near City College. Dr. Irving wouldn't be hard to find if the card was legitimate. If it wasn't, I was a prize-winning sucker.

Such morbid thoughts were disturbed by an enfilade of gravel against my pants leg from the hearse as it passed at a fair clip through the big gates. Following it was the limousine with old McDavitt sitting erect and composed in the back seat. He didn't even give me a nod, but I didn't have much time to nurse my wounded pride. The taxi from San Francisco was hot on the Caddy's tail, and Royster was hanging out of one back window, shaking his fist and shouting: "Get laid, you old bag! They ought to bury you, too!"

Which I thought was pretty rude, since he was addressing the mother of the deceased.

13

THAT SAME OLD PERSON WAS COMING TOWARD ME RIGHT then at a pace only slightly slower than a good half-miler on a straight stretch. She had her long, black dress held up around her knees, and she was eating up ground at about two yards a stride. I was between her and the gate. My two choices were either to get out of her way or get run down.

I took the coward's way out and cut slightly to the left, at the same time saying, "Mrs. Barton?"

She wheeled around at me, causing a small dust storm with her upraised skirts. "You a reporter too?" she demanded.

If I had been, I wouldn't have admitted it. But I could tell the truth. "No," I said, bringing out the buzzer again. "I'm a detective." That didn't seem to impress her either.

"You sure?" she said. "You don't look like any cop to me. Those reporters," she added, "I wouldn't piss on the best part of them. They ask you a whole lot of stupid questions, and then they go off and leave you at the end of creation. Bastards, they are. Real bastards. And McDavitt's no better. He demands payment in advance and then claims to have an urgent call to make in Hillsborough. Hillsborough!" she repeated, spitting on the toe of my shoe.

"So you're stuck," I said, cutting to the heart of the matter.

"Son," she countered, "I'm never stuck as long as I've got these." She held up a fair-sized foot in what looked like a badly dyed bowling shoe. The sole was already beginning to curl back at the toe. She'd be barefoot before she got a mile. "And this." She stuck a thumb like a small baked potato in front of my face. "I'll be back in West Pittsburg before you could finish eating a banana split."

"West Pittsburg?" West Pittsburg was a godforsaken little town at least fifty miles away over on the other side of the bay at the mouth of the Sacramento River. Somehow I could imagine her in dusty mourning weeds hitching all that way.

"Close enough to it," she said. "I've got a little place on the Contra Costa Canal." She fixed me with a narrow gaze. "You wouldn't be going out in that direction, would you?"

"Not intentionally," I said, "but I'll make you a deal. I'll give you a ride home if you'll tell me a bit about your daughter."

She gave me a bit more of the deadeye, thought it over, and then looked down at her feet. "You sure you're a cop?"

"Ex," I said, giving her a closer look at the buzzer. "And I don't like reporters any better than you do." That went down well with her, so she decided to take a chance.

"Where's your car?"

I pointed to the Morris, and her face dropped a bit. Maybe she'd expected a Cadillac like the one she'd come in. Tough luck. Watching her face, I could see that she was weighing her chances of getting a better ride hitching. Then she shrugged.

"Okay, Goodey," she said. "But could you put the top up? The sun gives my complexion fits."

I doubted whether anything short of a flame thrower could do that, but I wrestled the fragile old top up and we set off for the Bayshore Freeway and West Pittsburg via San Francisco. Behind us the caretaker was struggling to shut the gates.

Before I could start asking questions, she undid a couple of buttons, loosened something around her middle, kicked off the bowling shoes, sighed contentedly, and asked me, "Why do you care who killed my daughter?"

She looked tough enough to stand a little truth, so I said: "I don't really, but the person I'm working for would like to know. He has his reasons."

"Who'd that be?"

"Nobody you would know," I said. "I'm supposed to be asking the questions here. Are you sure you're not a newspaper reporter?"

That tickled her, and after a crackly laugh she said: "I'll tell you one thing for sure. Her name wasn't really Tina D'Oro."

"I figured as much," I said. "What was it?"

"If you know so damned much," she said acidly, "figure that out, too." She didn't like smart alecks.

"Sorry," I said.

After a long pause to let me know I was on probation, she sniffed loudly and said: "Olga. Olga Dombrowitz. The Olga was after a dancer I once saw in a show over in Concord. Olga Samovar, it was. Did a little bit from Swan Lake."

"Funny how your Olga turned out to be a dancer too."

"You may call standing up on a bar jiggling your tits dancing," she said sharply, "but I don't. No, Olga could have been a dancer, but she was too lazy. Bone idle."

"Where'd the Dombrowitz come from?"

"Mr. Dombrowitz," she said, "was my first husband. He was the headwaiter on a boat that used to go up and down the river between Sacramento and San Francisco. He knew every member of the state legislature by his front name. We lived in Pittsburg then, and I used to take Olga down to the dock so that she could wave at her daddy. The captain would do the old 'Shave and a haircut—two bits' on the steam whistle for her."

"What happened to Mr. Dombrowitz?"

"World War II. He was too old for the army so the damned fool signed on with the merchant marine. Ran into a torpedo someplace out in the Atlantic, and there wasn't enough left to send home. That was early in 1943."

As sad as the demise of Mr. Dombrowitz was, I couldn't help noticing something that didn't seem to jibe. "Nineteen forty-three?" I said. "How—"

"You're surprised, aren't you? How old did you think Olga was?"

"Twenty-five," I said, "maybe twenty-six."

"Wrong!" she said triumphantly. "Olga would have been thirty-five come this November. The seventeenth. She fooled everyone, she did. Did you see her laying in that fancy coffin at the church?" I said I'd missed that experience.

"Well, I'm telling you right now she could have passed for a girl of twenty and one. She never looked so good in her life. Whatever that McDavitt did to her, he did the right thing. Downright beautiful. That's what got me to howling there at the grave. I'm a pretty hard old devil..." She took a sideways look at me to see if I was going to contradict her, then she shrugged. "But when I saw her looking almost as young as she did when she graduated from John C. Fremont Junior High, I just went to pieces."

She rummaged through a handbag that had cost the lives of at least two alligators and brought out a tattletale-gray man's handkerchief just in case she had another attack. But it didn't come.

"Mrs. Barton," I suggested, "why don't you just go back to the time Tina—somehow, I can't get used to calling her Olga—

graduated from junior high school and take it right up to the present. I'll ask you a question or two if some occur to me."

She wasn't too happy about me calling the shots, but the old lady wriggled herself into a more comfortable position, took something fuzzy with lint from the bottom of her purse, stuck it in the side of her jaw, and started talking. At the Bay Bridge toll booth she opened the big purse again and dived in for a good rummage until I'd paid the toll, but mostly she just talked. She'd had some practice; I could tell.

Leaving out the more convoluted subplots and tortured rhetoric, the truth seemed to be that Tina was born on the outskirts of Pittsburg a couple of years before the war. After Mr. Dombrowitz was torpedoed, a series of "stepfathers" came and went. Mrs. Barton seemed to remember most of them and recited their names with some relish: Mr. Roper, Mr. Hawkins, Mr. Hufnagel, that son of a bitch Charlie Ramond, Mr. Gilliam. But Tina grew up just like other little girls in the East Bay until she graduated from junior high school.

That was the extent of her formal education, and it qualified Tina for a choice spot behind the candy counter at Kress's in Antioch. P. D. Zimmerman, the manager, gave her in fairly rapid sequence a promotion to lipsticks, a ten-cents-an-hour raise, a baby, and enough money to go to San Francisco for an abortion.

Tina never came back, at least not for any amount of time. Oh, a couple of years later she did come home to stay long enough to have a baby. It seemed that her first experience with an abortionist had put her off that gentle art for life. But then as soon as the stitches were removed and the baby was hooked on the bottle, Tina—she was still calling herself Olga—had gone off again, leaving behind the baby, a hundred and ten dollars in cash, and an expensive pigskin suitcase.

"What happened to the baby?" I asked, as we drove through the tunnel heading for Orinda.

"It didn't live," she said, taking a good grip on the hanky again. "The poor little bugger. The winter after Olga went back to San Francisco it took down with gastro—gastro-something-or-other and just wasted away. We had the doctor out, but it just got thin like a little skeleton. One morning I found it dead." She started snuffing in the big handkerchief. "I haven't thought about that baby in years."

"How did Tina take it?" I asked to get her off the morbid reminiscences and back on the story.

Mrs. Barton threw back her head and sniffed deeply. "Just like she took everything else," she said. "Dead easy. She sent me twenty-five bucks to buy a little gravestone with and didn't bother to come home for six months."

She looked at the handkerchief again as if wondering whether to have another go at it, but then stuffed it back into the dead alligator. "You're certainly a nosy bastard," she said.

"It's my job. After that, did you see much of Tina?"

"Olga," she corrected. "She didn't take the name of Tina D'Oro until maybe five years ago. No, she didn't come back much. But every so often there she'd be. She was onto something good in those days. She was always dressed smart and driving a new car."

"Did she ever tell you his name?" I asked.

"Whose name?"

'The man who was providing all those smart clothes and new cars. Did she happen to mention who he was?"

She looked across the front seat at me like a turkey hen that'd been run down in a dusty street by a bread van. "She didn't tell me," she said, "but I found out. He was crazy about her, he was, and he couldn't let her be away for even a couple of days without writing to her."

"And you snooped."

"Yes, I snooped. Isn't that what you're doing?"

She had me there. "Are you going to tell me his name?"

"What are you going to do for me?"

"I might find out who stabbed your daughter to death, in case you're interested. Might even get him punished."

"How's that gonna help me?" she demanded. Then she lapsed into a bout of subdued grumbling as we pulled into Walnut Creek.

The old woman hadn't seen Tina in nearly a year, and it was pretty clear that she hadn't any more idea who killed her than I did. Still, if she'd give me the name of old Sugar Daddy, it might lead somewhere. Or nowhere. We drove more or less silently through hilly East Bay country until I saw a sign that said Contra Costa Canal.

"You'll have to direct me from here," I told her. "I'm a stranger in these parts."

"Sometimes I wish I was, too," she said, but she directed me down a dirt and gravel road along the canal bank past a couple of tarpaper shacks. At the sound of my car, occupants of various sizes and sexes emerged into the glaring sunshine to wave Mrs. Barton home like a returning duchess. She acknowledged their greetings with sullen grace.

"Lot of no-account people live along the canal these days," she muttered, hinting at genteel days long past.

We bumped across a railway line which crossed the road at a right angle, turned sharply to follow the canal perhaps fifty yards, and then came to a dead end at a half-submerged pier jutting out into the canal. There, sitting at the end of the line, was an old, red-brown Southern Pacific caboose which had been converted into a house. A line of limp laundry ran down to a pole from the high poop deck at one end. An old geezer dressed in a railman's striped overalls looked up at the car from his calabash pipe without hostility but with no great enthusiasm, either.

"You made good time," he told Mrs. Barton, snapping up the lid on a turnip-sized watch hung on a finely wrought gold chain.

"This fella's name is Goodey, Jim," the old woman said in a completely different tone from the one she'd used with me. "He says he's some kind of detective looking into Olga's death." Then she said to me, "This is Mr. Barton," as if introducing me to the Duke of Earl.

Barton was a fine-faced old man not far off seventy, with a geometrically precise trainman's mustache. He had a faint gray powder of beard on his weathered cheeks which left him just short of needing a shave. He'd probably figured out just how long a retired railroad man could go between shaves without looking like a bum. When he did shave it would be with a straight razor. Barton looked me over with fathomless gray eyes that gave away nothing.

"Have you got anything in the way of credentials, Mr. Goodey?" he asked politely. I came up with the brand-new private operative's license, and he looked it over with an eye that could spot a phony cargo manifest at fifty feet. He didn't hurry, but read it all and then handed the card back to me. "You're new to the game, aren't you?"

"Yes," I said. "But I was on the force in San Francisco for nearly fifteen years." That didn't make me a forty or forty-five-year man as he'd obviously been with the railroad. But it gave me a bit more credibility in his eyes.

"I'm Jim Barton," he said, giving me a tough old hand to shake. "I didn't know Olga at all. Only met her once just short of a year ago. But what can we do for you out here?"

"I met Mrs. Barton at the funeral," I said, "and on the way back here she mentioned that she might know the name of a man Olga lived with in the early years when she first left here for San Francisco. I'd find it useful to have that name."

"That right, Maggie?" Barton asked, turning his eyes on her. She wriggled under them like a schoolgirl. I swear she even blushed.

"I used to know that fella's name, Jim," she said, "but it's been a lot of years since then. If I've still got it around, it'll be in my box." She didn't seem to be too eager to produce it.

"Well," he said, "you just go up and root through that box until you find it. And while you're at it, make some tea. I'll entertain Mr. Goodey while you're gone."

We watched her climb up the iron steps into the main body of the caboose and disappear from sight. Then Barton gestured to a low bench, and we both sat watching rubbish float downstream in the murky brown canal water.

"You like being a private detective, Mr. Goodey?" Barton asked, relighting his big pipe with a puff of gray smoke.

"It's hard to say so soon," I answered, "but I don't think I will. There's too much uncertainty in it."

"Well," he said, "that may be, but let me give you some advice. No matter how much you don't like your job, it's better than being retired. When the time comes that somebody wants to retire you, you take that gun of yours—you're not wearing one, I see, but you've got one, I imagine?"

"Somewhere around," I said.

"You take that gun of yours and blow your brains out first before you let them retire you. That's my advice." He spat into the slow-moving canal.

"That's how much you like being retired, is it?"

"Yep," he said. "They gave me a watch, they gave me a fair little pension, and they even gave me this old caboose. But it don't make up for not having a job. Not half."

"And you don't have a gun?" I felt shamed to ask.

"I've got a gun, all right, a big, hawg-leg thing of a pistol. But I haven't got the guts to use it. And that's a hard thing to live with too."

"You'll manage somehow," I said, "and so will I when the time comes. Let me ask you something, Mr. Barton. What did you think of Olga?"

"Not much. As I say, she came out here maybe a year ago to see her mother. Seemed to me she was all tits and seventy-five-cent words. Tough as day-old hardtack on the surface and not much softer underneath. One thing stuck in my mind about her."

"What's that?"

"Ambition. She was maybe a hundred and twenty-five pounds of walking, talking ambition. She had the gimme's and gotta's so bad she couldn't sit still. She wasn't here any more than three hours before she was up and off. Wasn't any way at all that hanging around this dump was going to get her where she wanted to go."

"Where's that?"

"Somewhere, anywhere. You know, I told you I only met her once, but I've seen her since. About six months ago I was in San Francisco, and I found myself down in North Beach. I had some time to kill before I caught the bus, so I went into The Jungle for a drink and a peek at Olga at work. There wasn't much of a crowd, it being a Tuesday night, so I sat right up at the bar, and some girl with no shirt on took two dollars off of me for a shot of bad rye and a beer chaser. After a while Olga came on."

"And?"

"It wasn't worth the buck fifty, not even if I was half my age."

"Did she see you?"

"I doubt it. As far as I know, all she could see was herself in those big mirrors."

Just then, Maggie Barton came down the steps of the caboose with two mugs of steaming tea balanced on top of a rosewood writing box. She'd changed to an old pair of blue jeans and a checked cotton shirt and looked more like herself.

Old Barton and I took the mugs and made appreciative noises over the good, strong, milky tea. "Did you find the name?" Barton asked.

"Yes," she said, but she wasn't rushing to give it to me. She had her arms wrapped around the box as if it contained atomic secrets.

"Well?" said Barton impatiently. I couldn't have said it better.

"It does seem to me, Jim," she said, "that we ought to get something for it. This guy's probably making a fortune."

"Give it to the man, woman," he said in a voice that didn't take to argument.

"Oh, all right," she said, opening the box narrowly and throwing a pale-blue envelope in my lap. "This is fifteen years old, and he might not even be alive now."

That's logic for you: try to bargain a good price and then when you fail to get it, knock the merchandise. I picked the envelope out of my lap and saw that it was addressed to Miss Olga Dombrowitz at an address in West Pittsburg. I turned it over and in a fine Italic hand faded to a whispery gray was the name Antonio Scarezza.

She was right. I didn't know if Scarezza was still alive, either. But when I was cutting my teeth on a nightstick, he was the biggest man in the dock rackets. Only then he was called Tony Scar.

14

It was late afternoon by the time I'd driven back to San Francisco. It seemed just about the right time to go see Doc Irving, the weeping physician. His office wasn't hard to find. It was in the heart of the Ocean Avenue shopping district in an anonymous, chlorine-green building set back from the sidewalk and guarded by two sick-looking palm trees. A small brass plate next to the bell told me his name was still Fletcher Irving, M.D., and that he saw patients By Appointment Only. That's all.

I gave the bell a discreet push, and after a short interval a woman's fuzzy voice came out of a small grille at about Adam's apple level: "Yes? Who is it?"

"The name is Goodey," I said, stooping slightly. "I have an appointment with Dr. Irving."

There, was a short, muffled consultation about that, and then a man's voice said, "This is Dr. Irving, Mr.—?"

"Goodey," I told the grille, "Joe Goodey. I'm the detective you met earlier today at Holy Martyrs Cemetery. You said to come see you."

Doc Irving switched off, and I could tell that he was wondering how to get rid of me. He didn't have a chance.

"Mr., ah, Goodey," his voice crackled, "couldn't you—"

"No, I couldn't, Dr. Irving," I said in a very loud voice, "and there's a crowd of people out here on the sidewalk beginning to wonder why I'm yelling at your front door." There really wasn't much of a crowd, but I could guarantee to get one in a hurry.

After a short pause for thought, he said, "Very well, come up then." A buzzer sounded, and the thick, oak-veneer door cracked open.

The staircase going straight up from the front door was carpeted in something like cashmere, and the wallpaper was that nubby stuff rich doctors and society matrons seem to favor. The stairway lamp was a discreet fleur-de-lis shape with a soft light which would be flattering to less-than-perfect complexions.

Standing at the top of the stairs was Dr. Irving. He was wearing a smart, off-white surgical coat and looked considerably improved over the last time I'd seen him. His eyes were only slightly red at the edges, and his homely, youthful face with its cartoon-button nose looked most professional and even suave. He gave me a shy smile. I didn't know what to do with it, so I gave it back to him.

"Mr. Goodey," he said, blocking the door behind him at least semi-intentionally, "what can I do for you?" He put out a hand in a gesture which was half greeting and half stiff-arm. I took his hand, smiled winningly, and, without being too obvious about it, maneuvered it and him through the doorway and into the anteroom of his offices. It looked as plush as the stairs, maybe a little better, and a girl was sitting in it on an expensive leather sofa looking at us.

She was perhaps twenty-seven years old, dark-haired, and well-built in a modest way. She had the face of a girl who'd lived a lot but hadn't let it get her down. There was something in her eyes—I couldn't make out the color in the dead light of the anteroom—that said she knew what she wanted. She didn't say anything. Neither did I, but I filed her away for future reference.

Irving didn't look too happy to have me cluttering up his place, but he didn't offer to throw me down the stairs, either. So I quietly stood there waiting for his next opening. Pretty soon the tension got to him.

"What do you *want*, Mr. Goodey?"

"I want to know what your relationship was with Tina D'Oro and why you were so broken up at her funeral today. And if she meant so much to you, why didn't you join us at the graveside instead of lurking out there in the bushes?"

That was a lot all at once for him, and he reddened up and looked as though he was going to brim over again. But he swallowed instead, raised up on his toes a little and did his best to look me in the eye. That's not really a very big job, but the doc wasn't up to his best form.

"I was Miss D'Oro's doctor," he said, making the job sound like a combination of royal physician and grade-A wizard.

"So?" I said in my most obtuse manner. Nothing brings out the blabbermouth in some people like a dumb, uncomprehending cop. I shifted my position slightly so that I could watch both Irving and the girl at the same time. Her face, not conventionally pretty but handsome in a slightly aquiline way, was calm enough, but she wasn't missing a thing.

The doctor cleared his throat portentously. "Mr. Goodey," he said, "did you ever see Tina D'Oro dance?"

"Once or twice."

"What did you think of her body?" He asked the question casually enough, but there was a lot behind it. Any way you look at it, it was a queer question for a doctor to ask. I didn't want to rush into an answer which might put him off, so I tried to look as if I were carefully phrasing my reply. He couldn't wait.

"I mean," Irving said, "do you think she had a beautiful body?"

He couldn't have given me the answer more plainly without using ventriloquism, so I said: "Of course. She had the most beautiful body I've ever seen." Which was a lie, but a useful one. As far as Dr. Irving was concerned, I'd spoken the magic words. I was in. His face lost a lot of tension and relaxed into what must have been his usual, slightly dopey expression of friendliness. And behind it in his doggy eyes was the gleam of the true believer, the holder of truth. He was going to let me in on something.

"Mr. Goodey," he said, "I created Tina D'Oro's body."

I was working overtime trying to get an expression of amazed incredulity on my face when he followed up with: "Of course, Tina was an early effort, in some ways quite a primitive effort—almost crude—but nonetheless I am proud of my creation. As you may have guessed, I am what is popularly called a plastic surgeon." I had guessed, actually. "I created Tina's body just as surely as Michelangelo created 'La Pietà.' Surely you can understand how I felt this afternoon when Tina was lowered into her grave."

I looked understanding, but this was wasted on the mad doctor. He was caught up in his own enthusiasm. He put an urgent hand on my sleeve. "Come," he said, "would you like me to show you how I made Tina D'Oro what she was?"

Now there was a question that had only one possible answer. "Yes, please," I said, like a good boy.

But Doc Irving had already taken my answer for granted. He signaled the girl to follow and turned to open the door to the inner sanctum. "Follow me," he said, "and I will show you something truly remarkable."

I politely let the girl go first, for which she didn't show much gratitude, and followed. If I'd been expecting Dr. Frankenstein's laboratory with flashing lights and gurgling test tubes, I'd have been disappointed. Dr. Irving's wonder factory turned out to be a large, smooth, pastel room like the conference room of a successful advertising agency. It featured a large, round slab-of-marble table surrounded by four bucket chairs on pedestals and a wall lined with brass-handled cabinets and drawers of various sizes. There was no sign of an operating table.

Irving motioned me and the girl, who hadn't said a word since we'd had that chat over the intercom, into two of the bucket seats and opened a large cabinet door on the slightly curved wall. A sixteen-millimeter projector slid out on a hinged platform, and the doctor rummaged through a low drawer, full of things which clanked metallically. The recessed lights began to dim, and a patch of white light sprang to a flat, beige wall across from where we were sitting. Movies.

Irving expertly threaded a reel of film, pushed a button, and a jumble of numbers flickered on the screen. Then the hand-lettered title: "Miss Tina D'Oro—February 1968." The doc ought to get together with Fat Phil. They could make a fortune. But the Tina who flashed on the screen, looking nervous in front of a dead-white wall, wasn't the Tina I'd known or the one they'd buried that day. She didn't look much younger, perhaps even a little older in a strange way. The eyes weren't exactly dewy with innocence, but there was something softer in them that had since crystallized. The face was vaguer, less formed, and her mouth hung a little slackly in contrast with the lush tautness we all knew. It might have been another girl entirely, but one thing told me it wasn't. There was a flickering hunger in the face that was unmistakable.

I was looking at the screen past the girl's face, and there was enough light for me to see that what she was seeing was hitting her hard. Some of the control had gone out of her face. She was blinking fast, but couldn't take her eyes off the screen.

"This was Tina D'Oro the first day she came to me," Irving said behind us in a narrator's voice. The camera zoomed up on Tina until from the waist up she filled the small screen. The color of the image was hard, slightly brighter than reality, and Tina's crudely applied make-up made her look like a slightly depraved doll. A pointed pink tongue touched the corner of her mouth. There was doubt in her eyes.

Then, obviously responding to an order from behind the camera, Tina reached down with disembodied hands and began to pull a frilly, green blouse up over her head, revealing a black lace brassiere that was in no danger of overflowing. She shook her short, bleached hair as the blouse came off, and the hand carrying the blouse dropped off the screen. Her eyes responded to another command. She reached up behind her with both pale arms. The black brassiere started to fall, retained only by thin shoulder straps.

"Stop!" The voice was a pain-filled shriek, and it came from the girl who'd been sitting at the table with me. But now she had jumped up between table and screen, blocking the beam of light from the projector. The mottled image of Tina dropping her brassiere flickered wildly on her face, neck, and blouse. "Stop it!" she repeated. "Turn it off!"

The image died, the ceiling lights came on, and Doc Irving was revealed standing next to the projector, looking startled and scared.

"Now, my dear," he said in a shocked voice, "I'm only—"

The girl turned on him. "Can't you just leave her alone?"

she demanded. "She's dead. Isn't that enough?" She looked ready to brain Irving with his own projector. I'd expected to see tears, but her eyes were as dry as moon dust, with a dull glint that was more painful than tears.

"Now, Miss Springler," the doc said, "now—"

Irma Springler. A piece of the puzzle slipped into place.

"No," she said with finality, raising her arms slightly as if to block further attempts at projection. Some of us were going to have to ask for a refund.

"Leave Tina alone," she continued. "If you've got to show this"—she shot an unloving look at me—"this man your art, show him on me." She reached up behind her neck, did something to the collar of an apricot-colored, tailored silk blouse, and pulled it smoothly over her head. She wasn't wearing a brassiere, but the effect wasn't so much sexy as clinical. She dropped her hands to her sides, wrists turned slightly toward Dr. Irving, and waited passively, looking at nothing.

Irving cleared his throat of something only slightly smaller than the Boulder Dam and generally got a grip on himself. "Perhaps," he said, as if it had been his own idea, "that would be a better method. After all, the techniques of today bear no resemblance to those of 1968." Professionalism was flowing back into his voice and manner. He turned the ceiling lamp up bright and stepped toward Irma Springler, moving to her side like a professor of anatomy. She could have been a mannequin for his purposes.

"As you can see, Mr. Goodey," he began, "there is nothing basically wrong with Miss Springler's breasts." He put a small, neat hand under one breast and handled it as a good grocer would a ripe avocado. I was watching Irma's face, but she didn't know he was there. "They are well-formed, erect, of a size generally consistent with the rest of her body. Many a girl would consider herself blessed to have such a pair of breasts."

Or even one. I couldn't argue with him so far, but I was sure that the nugget was yet to come. It did.

"However," he continued, "they are hardly adequate for the line of endeavor which Miss Springler now intends to undertake. As you may not know, I have been asked to enable her to carry on where Tina left off as the starring topless dancer of The Jungle Club."

That I didn't know. I looked at Irma Springler questioningly, but she was not giving any answers. She was somewhere else.

"And so," Irving said, "I am going to use my skills as a surgeon to create for her perfect breasts—no, magnificent breasts. As you may have gathered," he said, his voice going a bit lumpy again, "I was very proud of what I had done for"—he rolled his soft eyes at Irma, but she didn't flinch—"Tina D'Oro. But that is past history. As beautiful as Tina's body was, it was achieved with technology which is now as dated as the piston-powered airplane."

He was off and running now, a stereotypical mad scientist itching to get down to the nitty-gritty of his black art but wary of giving away his holy secrets.

"Of course," Irving carried on, his left hand still holding Irma's right breast as if it were a laboratory beaker, "I can't expect you to understand the fine points of reconstructive surgery. But basically I will begin just as I did on Tina." He was free and easy with the name now. Irving was the complete pro, as if he were describing past triumphs with a few of the boys at the Surgeons' Club.

"I shall begin"—his right forefinger became a scalpel—"with an incision here." He traced a semicircular line along the lower edge of Irma's nipple. Her face didn't show a thing, but I could feel the blade bite. "This, of course, will enable me to insert the implant which will result in augmentation of the breast. Not just augmentation, but a result so totally lifelike that the patrons of The Jungle, you, or even Miss Springler will not be conscious that her breasts are not totally her own."

Doc Irving was really getting into it. He was going to dazzle me with science. "You see, Mr. Goodey," he continued, confident of my unswerving attention, "the crucial element of such an operation is the character and consistency of the implant used. In the past a number of substances have been used with mixed results, among them silastic sponge, saline solution, gel sacs, microporous sponge. One of the earliest methods was to use excess subcutaneous fat from the patient's own body." He smiled winningly. "But I can't see that Miss Springler has much excess body fat, can you?" I shook my head gravely, trying not to feel too much like a peeping Tom or a cattle inspector.

"A recent trend," he went on, "has been to use liquid silicone. This has produced some spectacular results, but it is extremely doubtful medically. Silicone in that form has an unfortunate tendency to travel and can be absorbed into certain organs with serious results, including carcinoma." At that word Irma grimaced involuntarily, and I didn't feel so well myself.

"I myself have never used silicone," Irving said. "And in recent months I have perfected a completely new type of implant which I will employ in my work on Miss Springler." He tried to look wise and secretive. "Of course, I can't reveal the exact nature of this implant, but I can assure you that the technique and material I will use is far in advance of anything the field has yet seen. Confidentially, I have every hope of getting into the textbooks with this one. I—"

"That's great," I interrupted, "but it doesn't really help me much with what I've come to see you about. I'm not a measurable distance closer to finding out who killed Tina D'Oro."

The mad doctor looked sheepish, but Irma Springler came out of her trance and snapped, "Who asked you to find out who killed Tina?" She was getting back into the tailored blouse, and quite gracefully too.

"That's none of your business," I said politely, "but if you're just about finished here, I've got some questions for you about Tina D'Oro."

We locked eyes for a moment. Then something softened in her hard gaze, and she said, "I'm through here right now, and if you're driving toward North Beach, we can talk." She turned to Irving. "Are you all set to begin on Monday morning, Doctor?"

"All set, Miss Springler," he said, smoothly professional, "if you are. I'll see you here at ten in the morning."

"I'll be here." She was headed out of the laboratory, and I couldn't think of any reason not to follow her. The doc tagged along too.

"You'll be around, Doctor," I asked him, "in case I can think of any intelligent questions to ask you?"

"I'll be around, Mr. Goodey," he said. "I live at the top of this building. I'll try very hard to think of something to help you in your inquiries, but my relationship with Miss D'Oro was strictly professional."

"You do that," I said. "I'd like to come around sometime and see the rest of that film."

He gave me a warning frown, but Irma Springler was heading out of his office door, and I didn't have much time to feel gauche. She was quick on the stairs, and outside near the brass plate I caught up with her, looking slightly impatient. The big door closed behind us.

"Let's get out of here," she said, a bit more friendly. "That place gives me the creeps."

I walked over to the Morris parked at the curb, and Irma drifted along at my side. She slid quite willingly into the cracked leather passenger seat. I got in behind the steering wheel and waited for an opening in the flow of Saturday evening traffic.

"I'm sorry I was so snappy in there," she said as I got the car out into the street. "The last few days have been hell for me."

"Don't apologize. I have a tendency to wade in, stomping all over people's sensibilities. I'm cursed with a one-track mind. I should apologize to you. Do you feel up to answering a few questions while we drive, or would you rather wait?"

"Go ahead," she said, letting her head rest against the seat back and nearly closing her eyes. "I want to help you all I can."

By then I was past City College, and we joined the early dinner crowd on the freeway headed downtown. I pulled into the slow lane and drifted gently with the big trucks and old crocks like my own. "You were Tina's best friend?" I asked.

"I think so," she said. "Tina didn't have many friends. I met her last autumn when a girl friend of mine brought her around, and Tina asked me if I'd do her hair."

"You're a hairdresser?"

"Not really. It's a hobby of mine, and Tina claimed she'd never before found anybody who could do her hair just right. I didn't believe her at first, but Tina had a way of getting what she wanted."

"If you're not a hairdresser, what do you do for a living?"

"Nothing," she said, "right now, but until the end of May I was teaching at Marin Junior College."

"Teaching what?"

"Basic English, history, a bit of sociology. Mostly to freshmen."

"It's a long way from Basic English to the stage of The Jungle," I said, trying not to sound too scornful about it.

"Yes," she said, and I thought she sounded rueful. Irma was silent for about half a dozen of those tall, arc-lighted poles along the James Lick Memorial Freeway. Then she spoke, and the light was so dim that I could barely catch her features out of the corner of my eye. "Look," she said seriously, "can I trust you?"

Now, there was a good question. Could Irma Springler, teacher turned go-go dancer, trust Joe Goodey, ex-cop and would-be private detective? I hoped I hadn't waited too long before I said: "I think so. All I want from you is information that might help me find out who murdered Tina." That sounded altruistic, but it was true.

"That's good," she said, "because that's all I want from you too. If you're working for Phil Franks, I'm in trouble, because I have no intention of ever dancing for him at The Jungle. I want to find out who killed Tina, and I figure that the best way is from the inside."

"You'll even let Doc Irving try his magic formula on you?" I asked. That seemed to me to be going a bit far, even for a best friend.

"If I have to," she said in a neutral tone. "But I think I can stall Irving for a while. Phil will be harder to handle, so I've got to work fast. We both want the same thing, Joe. Do you think we could work together?"

That was the best offer I'd had all day, which gives you an idea of the quality of the offers I'd been getting. Unless Irma killed Tina herself, she probably knew as much about the murder as I did. Which wasn't very much. But I didn't have much to lose.

"I don't see why not," I said. "I can't tell you who I'm working for, and other than that I don't know a hell of a lot more than you do. Probably less. But maybe we can do something together. Why don't you start by telling me something I don't know?"

"All right," she said in a voice full of hidden aces, "I will. I know that Tina was having an affair with Mayor Kolchik."

This hot tidbit was supposed to make me fall out of the car

and swallow my tongue. In order not to disappoint Irma too much, I managed a long, low whistle meant to convey the impression of surprise.

It didn't.

"You knew that already," she said accusingly, like a child whose riddle had flopped.

"You're right," I said. "But all the same it's very interesting that you know it. How is that?"

"Tina had no secrets from me," Irma said positively.

"She must have had at least one," I said. "And that's who was mad enough at her to stab her to death."

"That's what I can't figure out," Irma said, "unless..."

"Unless Tina did have some secrets from you," I said. "Do you think it's possible that she could have been running an entirely different game that you knew nothing about? How good an actress was Tina? For instance, could there have been another lover besides Kolchik? One she didn't tell you about?"

The high beams of an oncoming car illuminated her face enough for me to see that Irma didn't like the idea. Her face went rigid, and the high cheekbones stood out in relief. Then the car's light was gone.

"No," she said in a voice that was calmer than her face had shown. "I'd swear it. The mayor was the only man in Tina's life. If there'd been another, I'd have had to know."

"What about Tony Scar?"

"What about who?" She wasn't faking it.

"Tony Scarezza. He used to be a big man on the docks. He was Tina's lover some years back. Did you know that she'd had a baby about fifteen years ago? Scarezza's baby. And it died young over at Tina's home in the East Bay?"

She was silent for a moment. Then Irma spoke: "You may have known Tina to talk to, Joe," she said, "but one thing you didn't know about her was that for Tina there was no yesterday, only today and tomorrow—mostly tomorrow. I didn't know about the baby or this Tony Scar person because for Tina they didn't exist. To Tina, yesterday was something you threw away with last night's paper. She was through with it, and it didn't matter."

"What did matter to Tina?" I asked.

"Her career," Irma answered after thinking carefully, "and her friends."

"And who were her friends besides you?"

Irma had to think that one over hard. I let her do it in peace as we plowed toward downtown San Francisco. We were just negotiating the link with the Embarcadero when she said: "There weren't any, really, I guess, unless you count Dr. Irving and maybe Phil Franks. But Dr. Irving was mostly concerned with keeping her body in shape. And Phil—I don't know exactly what Phil was. Sometimes Tina talked about him fondly; other times he was just a money-grubbing fat man. Tina knew a lot of people at other clubs on the street, but no one I'd really call a friend. Maybe Kolchik was a friend. I don't know."

Neither did I, and I wasn't getting much closer to finding out. It looked as if Kolchik didn't have any better eye for detectives than for girls. For all I knew, Johnny Maher had Tina's killer hog-tied in the basement of city hall.

We rolled down the Broadway off ramp.

15

"Are you hungry?" I asked Irma as we crept along in the tentative beginnings of what would later turn into the nightly traffic jam. "We could continue this over dinner."

She agreed, and a few minutes later we were being seated in a rear booth at Hungry Joe's by Mario, the headwaiter. Mario made up for being incredibly handsome by oozing an oily hospitality which always made me feel faintly in need of a steam cleaning.

"The veal tonight, m'sieur and m'selle," he said, "is exquisite. Besides, I've been asked by the chef to move it if at all possible." Save me from honest headwaiters. I told Mario to send us two Kahluas over crushed ice and promised to give the veal every consideration.

The drinks arrived, and I was about to beam back in on Irma with what I hoped would be pertinent questions. She'd gotten her nose stuck into the short, chunky glass of dark-brown coffee liqueur. When she came up for air with a sliver of ice on her lower lip, I was all set with a sure-fire winner. But just then

George, the barman, caught my eye with a fancy bit of cocktail bar semaphore. He looked as if he meant it.

"Sorry," I said, pushing back from the table and standing up. "Somebody seems to need to talk to me." I shoved my drink across the table toward her. "If you feel dehydration setting in, try this. I'll make it short."

George, the younger brother of a big-league baseball star, fancied himself a celebrity by genetic association, like the third son of an earl. Just then he was busy dazzling a motherly type with his way with a gin fizz, so I leaned against the polished oak bar and marveled. But quietly.

The fizz delivered and an unmotherly smile returned, George turned to me. "Hey, Joe," he said, "is it true that you're no longer a cop? That you're going to be a private detective?"

"Am a private detective, George," I corrected. "Am. And I've got the papers to prove it."

"Gee, that's too bad," he said, giving the bar an ellipsoidal sweep with a damp rag.

"How do you mean?"

"Now you won't be able to put your drinks on the tab. Mario won't deadhead anybody but the real thing."

"I'll try to survive the blow. Is that what you frantically signaled me over here to tell me?" I started to push myself away from the bar.

"Oh, no," he said. 'That's not it. It's something more important. Marley Phillips wants to see you."

Marley Phillips. In a B movie, that would have been a great spot for some theme music. Something with kettledrums. Instead, the only noise was the tinkle of ice cubes and the rustle of lies brushing up against broken promises.

"How do you know that?" I asked.

"He sent one of his mugs around this afternoon. An old guy

running on one lung and strong hair oil. He nearly passed out on the stairs."

"Did he say what Phillips wanted?"

"The way he was puffing and blowing," George said, "he was lucky to get that much out. That lad is a candidate for an iron lung. Are you going to see Phillips?"

"Maybe. But thanks for the message anyway." It doesn't pay to tell bartenders too much. I went back to the booth where Mario loomed over Irma like a walking lamp.

"I'm sorry," I told Irma, "but I've got to go see someone. It may be important." Mario turned his back discreetly, but his ears kept twitching. "You have dinner, and we'll meet later... say, at The Jungle at ten o'clock?"

"Okay," she agreed. "I'll see you there. In the meantime is there anything I can do"—she flicked her eyes at Mario's attentive back—"you know?"

"Not really," I said in a low voice. "Just keep your eyes and ears open and try to remember anything that might help." Without raising my voice or changing my tone, I said: "Mario, give this nice lady a good dinner. Anything but the veal."

"Yes, sir," he said, whirling around as if on ball bearings to gracefully take money from my hand. "I'll take good care of m'selle."

I was sure of that.

The car parker at the Mark Hopkins reluctantly accepted the Morris, and the doorman let me pass with no more than a look which said he didn't think much of my wardrobe, haircut, or career prospects. George had told me Phillips' suite number, so I gave the ramrod-stiff clerk behind the desk a miss and headed for the bank of elevators. I could feel his eyes on my back.

The elevator was soundless enough, but it stopped with a nasty jerk which brought back painful echoes of an old football injury to my left knee. I wondered whether I had sufficient grounds for a lawsuit. The closing door caught me wondering, and I had to strong-arm my way into the eighteenth-floor corridor.

The Mark Hopkins is a plush hotel. Not tacky-prefab posh like some of the newer high-rise mausoleums in San Francisco, but full of character like a sable coat with a moth-eaten lining. The corridor carpet wasn't an ankle-grabber, but its well-kept, timeworn veneer hinted that it had been trodden on by some of the quality.

The door to 18D, Phillips' suite, was slightly ajar. It had the air of a door that had never been anything else. I moved it a bit to see if the hinges were rusty. I edged through the door and stepped right out of the Mark Hopkins Hotel.

At first I didn't know where I was. I was dazzled by the pure drabness of the decor. Someone had walled off a section of the suite, forming a shallow, dark antechamber. The walls were the color of stale, diluted tobacco. The only decoration on them was a faded, flyblown Goodyear Rubber Company calendar. Some wiseacre had made a clumsy attempt to turn the Goodyear blimp into a tit. The carpet underfoot was thin to the point of near translucence and exuded dust with every footstep. The furniture—a cruel-looking library table, four broken-spirited chairs, and an ashtray on a bayonet stand—said back-alley abortionist.

But a half-glass door across the anteroom dimly lit from within said "M. Phillips, Private Investigations" in peeling bronze letters. "Knock First" warned a footnote on the door, so I did. I almost expected my knuckles to raise dust.

"Come in," said a heavy voice. "The door's not locked." I tried the knob and found that it was. I tried the knob a little harder, and it came off in my hand. "Come in, come in," said the same voice with distracted impatience. It came from a throat that had been well-cured with cigarette smoke.

"I'd sure like to," I said through the frosted glass, "but the door is locked, and I seem to have the knob in my hand."

Silence. Then the springs of a swivel chair squeaked pitifully, and footsteps—slow but not too heavy—came toward me. The door swung inward, and Marley Phillips filled most of the doorway.

It had been nearly five years since I'd seen Phillips, and he'd aged. Not radically, but gently, as if he were a shale boulder gradually being eroded by balmy winds and Pacific waves. He stood just under six feet tall, not slumped or bent but slightly telescoped, as if he'd been pressed down for a long time by a steady but not unbearable load. Phillips must have been close to seventy, and his face had the lines to prove it. But the brown eyes were bright and unclouded. Above them, his still-thick hair had gone gray-white.

When he opened the door, Phillips' face wore an expression I can only describe as martyred—tough, rude, likely to tell you to go to hell, but a martyr all the same. He was all set to hear about my problem.

Instead, I said, "Hello, I'm Joe Goodey."

The crown of thorns slipped from Phillips' brow, and the martyr was transformed into a professional. Old, tired, maybe past it, but a pro all the same. "Come in, Goodey," he said, turning back into the room. "Come in. Sorry I took so long to answer. I'm having a hell of a struggle with Steinitz. He's a stubborn son of a bitch."

As I followed him into the small, rectangular office, I swiveled my neck, trying to locate the son of a bitch. But all I could see was a room which equaled the antechamber in drabness. The only furniture in it was a blocky, heel-marked desk made of something which might have been wood once, a battered, slightly listing file cabinet with one drawer hanging open like a sleeping drunk's mouth, and an elderly hat rack groaning under the weight of an antique fedora with a turned-down brim. Rolled-down shades the color of dust dully reflected the light from a naked bulb dangling from the ceiling like a hanged man. On the far wall was a door with a frosted window labeled "Gents." A gooseneck telephone stood on the very edge of the desk as if it were thinking of jumping.

Phillips pointed me toward a chair and retired behind his desk. He instinctively fell into the pose of a man who'd seen everything—twice. Then I noticed that set up in the middle of a pool-table-green desk blotter was a fine ivory chess set on a board which looked like ebony. I don't know much about chess, but I could tell that somebody was getting the hell knocked out of him.

Phillips reached out and knocked over his sole bishop with a defeated hand. "If Steinitz hadn't been dead for over sixty years," he said, "I'd go step on his face." Then he looked up at me with eyes that might have seen the Crucifixion. "Now, what can I do for you?"

"I'm Joe Goodey," I reminded him gently. "You said you wanted to see me. George, the bartender at Hungry Joe's, gave me the message."

"Oh, yeah," he said. "Goodey. You're the cop who quit the force last week to become a private detective. I heard about it and wanted to have a talk with you. But first let's buy ourselves a drink. I think you'll find a bottle in the bottom drawer of that file cabinet." Yeah, he thought I'd find a bottle the way I think I'll find hands at the end of my arms. I turned, pulled open the drawer, and reached into its depths. My hand encountered and gripped something round, smooth and cool. I pulled out a quart bottle and set it on the blotter next to his busted chess game. The label said "Fine Canadian Rye, 12

Years Old," but the bottle was as empty as Miss America's smile.

Phillips had ducked down to a desk drawer and came up with a couple murky glasses. He took in the empty bottle with the expression of a condemned man whose reprieve from the governor turned out to be a singing telegram. He put the glasses down with a muted clunk. He raised his eyebrows wryly and said: "I forgot. They won't let me drink." A silence settled, and we sat there, me looking at nothing much and him fixing me with what was either a benevolent gaze or a disgusted stare.

Phillips pulled himself together manfully. "What I really want to know, Goodey," he said, "is are you going to turn out to be a shit-heel like most of the dicks in San Francisco, or are you trying to be a real private investigator?"

That must have been a rhetorical question, because I hadn't even opened my mouth to answer him when he was off and running again.

"I expect you know something about me, Goodey," he said, "but let me fill you in a bit. For nearly thirty years I was a private eye in Los Angeles. I never got rich, but I did all right. I never took a dirty dollar or chased too hard after a clean one. There are some old cops, retired now or maybe dead, who'd have told you I was a sneaky, crooked son of a bitch, but they'd have been wrong. I lied to a few cops in my day, held out on them. But I never sold a client out or betrayed a confidence. I've seen the inside of a cell on that account." All this he said almost to himself, but then Phillips looked up and got my eye in a hammerlock. "You know what I'm talking about, Goodey?" he demanded.

"I'm pretty sure I do."

"I'm not saying I haven't done things I shouldn't have," he went on. "I've killed men I wouldn't have had to if I'd been better at my job. I've slapped a few women around, but only when it was absolutely necessary. You ever hit a woman, Goodey?"

I riffled through my memory for a few moments and then said, "Not many, outside of my wife, that is."

Phillips didn't like that much, but he let it pass. "You married, then, Goodey?" he asked disapprovingly.

"I was," I said, "but the thing seems to have died a natural death. She's in New York."

He liked that better. "It's just as well," he said, the way surgeons don't mind talking about taking out your gall bladder. "I never met a married private detective who was worth a damn. Though there was one fellow once working out in the Valley who used to take his wife along on jobs. She'd sit in the car and knit while he worked. You have any idea what she was knitting?"

"You've got me."

"It turned out to be his shroud," said Phillips, not, I wouldn't be surprised, for the first time.

We both chewed that one over silently for a while.

Then Phillips started patting the breast pocket of a rumpled but very expensive sharkskin suit as if he were trying to put out a brush fire somewhere in his underwear. He stopped and looked up at me balefully.

"I used to get through forty to fifty Fatimas a day," he said, "some years back. But the sawbones said it was either cut down or put a down payment on a coffin. But that's my problem. What about you, Goodey? You pick up any jobs yet?"

"I've got a little something to keep me busy," I said modestly. "Would it by any chance have anything to do with the murder of Tina D'Oro?" he asked.

I put on my best poker face and looked back at him. "I've been wondering, Mr. Phillips," I said, "just what is behind that door with the 'Gents' sign."

"You're okay, Goodey," he said with a stiff smile. "You might just do eventually, though I never had much faith in cops turned private detective."

"I wasn't much of a cop," I said. But I was getting a bit sick of this routine, and I was curious. "If you don't mind me being nosy, Mr. Phillips, what the hell are you doing in this squalid mockup office in the middle of what must be a very nice hotel suite?"

I thought his eyes looked a little sad at the question.

"That's a very good question, Goodey," he said. "The truth is that I married a very rich woman. Not exactly just like that, mind you. I didn't just get up one morning and say: 'Phillips, you're getting too old and flabby to keep wearing your butt out on the LA freeways. Why not go out and find yourself a nice millionairess?'"

He paused, and when my look didn't exactly say, "Oh, yeah?" he went on.

"This woman," he said, "now Mrs. Marley Phillips, just sort of appeared one day. I hadn't seen her in over fifteen years, since we'd crossed paths on a job I did involving her family. Something clicked then, but I was relatively young and more than relatively stupid. I went back to knocking my brains out against other people's problems, and she went on to three or four more husbands. Then one day about ten years ago I looked up and there she was. I'd forgotten to turn on the buzzer in my outer office. Well, eliminating some of the cornier dialogue, we got married and moved up here. She can't stand the heat and smog."

"But," I said.

"Yeah," he grinned, "but it wasn't any good. She was happy as two clams, and I wasn't in any obvious pain. But something was wrong. I felt like a hound dog in a bubble bath. I kept looking at the marvelous views and getting morbid thoughts. So

I had some very expensive gentlemen go down to LA and bring back most of my office. I was lucky: they got there just ahead of the wrecker's ball. And now I sit here working on chess problems, reading a bit, and waiting for a knock on the door. I might still be in Los Angeles."

I started to ask him if the knock came often, but then the old gooseneck telephone started jangling, and Phillips snatched it with what I took to be just a bit of eagerness.

"Sure," he said, "in a minute." And he hung up.

"My wife," he said. "Dinner's ready." He dropped his big feet to the floor and stood up. "Thanks for coming by, Goodey," he said. "If I can ever do anything for you, you know where to find me." He turned toward the door with the frosted window.

I got an idea.

"You can help me, maybe," I said. "I'm trying to find somebody called Tony Scarezza. A guy who used to be a waterfront hood."

"Tony Scar?"

"That's right. Have you got any idea where I could find him?"

Phillips stopped with his hand on the open door. Through it I could see part of a rich, colorful suite. "Sure," he said. "Tony's out at Laguna Seca. Has been for at least three or four years. What do you want to see him for?"

"Marley, dear," a fruity old woman's voice called from the other room, "the soup is getting cold."

"Your soup's getting cold, Mr. Phillips," I said. "Thanks for the information." I walked out into the antechamber. It still looked crummy, and it was still empty. It always would be.

16

Laguna Seca. As I drove southwest on Market Street toward the old people's home beyond Twin Peaks, it occurred to me that this job had more old men in it than the Supreme Court.

At the entrance to the home, I found a gatekeeper sitting in an outsized telephone booth with a Zane Grey novel in his shiny lap. He looked like a retired mess sergeant—too young to die, too lazy to do anything.

"Sorry," he said without looking the least bit sorry, "visiting hours are two to five pee-em. You'll have to come back tomorrow." That took care of me, he figured, so he let his heavy eyes fall back to the book.

"This isn't social," I said. "It's business." I gave him a good look at the P.I. card. He must have had a firm grip on his chair because he didn't fall out of it.

"Visiting hours are still from two to five, stud," he said. "Try tomorrow. Sunday's a barrel of laughs around here."

"Sorry," I said. "I'm washing my hair tomorrow. Is there a

court of special appeal around here? Can you use that instrument to call someone with a bit more weight?"

I don't know what surprised him more: the thought that there might be someone more important than he was or the presence of a telephone in his booth. When he'd recovered, he picked up the telephone, dialed, and asked someone if he could speak to Dr. Chapel. There was a half-beat pause.

"Well, Christ on a fucking crutch," he shouted down the phone, "find him." He turned his head toward me. "Pardon my French," he said. "Until last February I was a chief bosun's mate, and it's hard to lose the habit."

"Don't tell me," I said. "Tell the operator."

"That wasn't the operator. It was the night head nurse. She—" Someone had come back on the telephone, and the chief slid his glass door closed so that they could have a private chat. While the gateman was working his jaws, I took a look around at what I could see in the darkness. Which wasn't much. Beyond the guard's booth in a grove of dead-black evergreens, pale towers of what must have been the Laguna Seca buildings stood out in shadowy relief against the moonless night. I felt glad I was going in for just a visit. That is, if I got in.

My friend slid the door open again.

"Can I see that card again, bud?"

I handed it to him, and the door shut again. He read what was on it to the party on the other end. The door opened, and he gave me back my card.

"Okay," he said, "go on through. Just keep taking bends to the left, and you'll see the main building on the left. Dr. Chapel will meet you there. Sorry it took so long. He was chewing my ass for being so rude to Mrs. Felony."

He read my expression.

"Felony. That's the name," he said. "Anyway, I'm to be

more polite to her in the future, and Dr. Chapel is waiting for you up at the ad building."

I admired his willingness to reform, thanked him, and got back into the Morris. He was right. A few left turns did find me coming into a half-moon drive in front of a dirty-white Victorian gingerbread mansion. A figure in crisp hospital whites was waiting for me on the bottom step of a short, wide flight of steps going to the main entrance. He came toward me as I got out of the car. He was taller than I, younger, handsomer, and no doubt richer. He walked bouncily as if he were dribbling a basketball.

"Mr. Goodey," he said, "I'm Dr. Chapel. What can I do for you?" We shook hands in a manly fashion, and I explained that I was there to have a short talk with Mr. Antonio Scarezza, a patient at the home. I started to add that unfortunately I couldn't divulge the nature of my inquiry, when he cut me off.

"Oh, I quite understand," he said understandingly. "I know that detective work requires a certain amount of confidentiality. I'm fairly conversant with the—uh—modus operandi."

Uh-oh. One of those. An amateur detective, or at least a wishful one. I wondered if I'd get to see his diploma from the Ajax College of Scientific Detection. I hoped not. But I know how to play the game, so I adopted a confidential tone of voice and leaned a little toward him.

"I greatly appreciate that, Doctor," I said man to man. "So often people misunderstand the nature of police work. You weren't by any chance a detective once yourself?"

"Oh, no," he said, more pleased than if I'd hung the Nobel Prize for Medicine around his neck. "When I was younger, I—well, I'd hoped—I'd wanted to major in criminology at college, but my father was a doctor, and—"

"Of course, of course," I said. "But you have kept up a keen interest in the profession, I imagine?"

"Oh, yes," he said, digging eagerly for his wallet and flapping it open to show me a Sheriff's Auxiliary shield, one of the toys the SF County Sheriff's office likes to hand out to law-and-order fans. They carry all the authority of a Chicken Inspector's badge. "I've worked quite closely with Sheriff Hallam. You know him, of course."

Of course. I'd once stepped on his foot in a City Hall elevator. We were old pals.

I tried to imply that with a look and came right to the matter at hand. Antonio Scarezza. "You're aware, of course, of Mr. Scarezza's background?" I said.

"Certainly, Mr. Goodey. We keep a fairly complete dossier on our—uh—residents here. You don't suspect, do you, that Mr. Scarezza has—er—retained his criminal connections even here at Laguna Seca?"

I put a mental finger alongside my nose and gave him a knowing look. "Let's just say, Doctor, that I'm pursuing a certain line of investigation. Is it possible for me to see Scarezza now?" I dropped the "Mr." purposely so that Dr. Chapel and I could enjoy a quiet moment of superiority over our unknowing quarry.

"I'm sure it is," he said agreeably, snapping a smart look at a gold watch in the dim light of a high, Victorian street lamp over our heads. "It's now the quiet hour in the wards, and pre-sleep drinks won't be served for about thirty-five minutes. Will that give you enough time?"

"I'm sure it will, Doctor," I said, shifting my weight toward the door in an effort to set him in motion, "if we can get to Scarezza pretty quickly." He must have been a basketball player once, because my feint set him in fluid, long-legged motion, and he was past me and heading for the stairs before I could move.

I caught up with Chapel at the top of the steps, and we

went in through the tall doorway in a dead heat. The foyer was all marble, thick Persian carpets, and paintings by obscure nineteenth-century artists with a penchant for seascapes. But I didn't have time to study them because Chapel cut sharply to his left and headed for a spiraling flight of carpeted marble steps. It was either go with him or foul him.

Midway up the first curve, just as I was beginning to feel the first inklings of oxygen starvation, Chapel resumed his just-between-us-detectives line. "I know Scarezza pretty well, Mr. Goodey," he said. "If you'd like, I could sit in on your interrogation." He flicked his eyes over at me shyly. "We could even work together, perhaps. I mean—what you call double-team him."

Yeah, I knew what he meant. He, the kindly, trusted physician, would be Dr. Nice. And I, the stranger, would be Mr. Nasty. Between us we'd wring the old man out like a bar rag.

"Thanks very much, Doctor," I said, trying to put a lot of regret in my voice, "but my client...well, you know how clients are." He knew, all right, just as I know all about old ladies too rich and too stubborn to die. He nodded conspiratorially, and his eyes told me he wasn't holding it against me personally.

On the elbow of the third upward twist of the stairs, we found ourselves facing a massive set of double doors with a sign over them reading "Norton Ward." Sitting at a small table to the side of the doors, reading an anatomy textbook, was a thin youth in a University of California letterman's jacket. We were all jocks around here. As we approached, the boy got up, but he didn't break his neck.

"Thompson," said the doctor, "this is Mr. Goodey. He has permission to see Mr. Scarezza until pre-sleep drinks are served. Will you take him in?" Chapel turned to me. "Good luck, Mr. Goodey. If I can be of any further help, I'll be downstairs in my office. Thompson will see that you find it." I could tell that he'd be lonesome if I didn't drop in, but I just smiled a bit grimly and gave him a firm handshake.

"I'll do that, Doctor," I said vaguely. "Thanks for all your help." He started back down the staircase like somebody's kid brother being left out of the big boys' games.

Thompson pulled open one side of the door. "This way, Mr. Goodey." The hallway we entered was wood paneled and lit discreetly. It wasn't much like a hospital, but it smelled of old men and bad chests and death.

"Nice place you've got here," I said, just to pass the time. "You planning to specialize in geriatrics?"

"Not me," he said without a smile. "I'm at the other end of the business—pediatrics. You meet a better class of young mothers, and your patients very seldom end up forgotten and drowning in their own spit. This is just a way of working my way through med school." As we passed a closed doorway on the left, a loud, monotonous murmur droned through the thick-looking door. Thompson checked his step and cocked an ear. So did I, and I heard a thick, strangled, old-man's voice warning someone called Madeline against the attentions of Mr. Battenborough. The drift of the monologue was that Mr. Battenborough was only after her fair white body and money, and she'd best listen to Dad and stay clear. The voice dropped to a muffled wheeze, and we moved on.

"What happened to Madeline?" I asked.

"She married Battenborough," Thompson said, "went through his money and the old man's, and ran away with a real estate man down in Menlo Park. I've never seen her, but Battenborough comes to see the old man twice a week."

As he said this, Thompson stopped in front of a door on the right and knocked softly. There was no answer, so he rapped more sharply.

"It's open," said a thin but unwavering voice.

Thompson turned the knob, and the door swung inward, revealing a fair-sized bedroom tricked out like a rich man's study. Flanking both sides of the large windows were library shelves loaded with thick volumes. A long desk with an extending-arm lamp commanded one wall, shoving a single bed into one corner as if it had been left there by mistake. The bed was unmade. Its usual occupant sat in a leather chair beneath a standing lamp, looking up at me with a sour expression.

He was a compact little guy. He looked hard but resilient, as if something hitting him would bounce back faster than it came. He had yellowish white hair, cut Jimmy Hoffa-style, and held in his hand a pair of tortoise half glasses that had been on his nose when the door opened.

His eyes weren't friendly, and they didn't melt much when Thompson said, "Mr. Scarezza, there's somebody here who would like to talk with you for a moment." He turned back to me. "Mr.—?"

"My name's Joe Goodey, Mr. Scarezza," I said. "I'm a detective, and..."

"Copper?" he said, his old face softening a bit with surprise.

"Ex. I'm private now. I..."

"Why should I want to talk to you?" he asked sharply. I was beginning to feel like a dog turd on his carpet.

So much for reverence for age, I thought, and put a bit of cutting edge on my voice. "You will when I tell you what I've come about. Do you want me to tell you or you *and* Dr. Kildare here?"

His dark gray eyes brightened a bit at that. Maybe nobody here bothered to get sharp with him. If I'd grabbed him by the front of his tweed robe and belted him in the chops, Scarezza would probably have given me a smile.

"Okay, Thompson," Scarezza said. "You can leave him

here." He sounded as if he were talking about a box of groceries.

"Right, Mr. Scarezza," said Thompson. "Pre-sleep drinks will be around in twenty-five minutes."

"I don't sleep, Thompson," the old man said. "You know that."

Thompson nodded professionally and beat it. He closed the door quietly behind him. I walked over to the desk, pulled a swivel chair out of the desk well, and sat on it facing Scarezza.

"It's true," he said, his voice a bit querulous in spite of himself. "The worst damn thing about getting old is you can't sleep. If it weren't for my books, I'd go nuts." He patted his book as if it were a favorite spaniel. Reading upside down, I could see that it was *The Dialogues of Plato*. I'd expected a bound volume of *Spicy Tales*.

"It all started the first year I was here," he said as if I'd asked him, "when some old broad of a night nurse saw that I couldn't sleep. She lent me her copy of Norman Vincent Peale's *The Power of Positive Thinking*. I was never much of a reader, but I got through it during that night. And it was such incredible bullshit that I thought I'd better see what else was going on in philosophy. And that led to this." He waved a hand at the book shelves, and my eye caught the names Descartes, Socrates, Sartre, Hegel. Not a Spillane in the lot.

"You learn anything from all that?" I asked.

"I don't know yet. A lot of it is garbage too, but it helps pass the time. Which is what we're wasting right now. What do you want from me, Goodey?"

"I'm looking into who killed Tina D'Oro."

That got a reaction, all right, but it wasn't one that I could catalogue. Maybe what I saw was the ripple of a memory coming to the surface from someplace deep and nearly forgotten. It didn't drag a lot of obvious pain with it.

"Yeah, Olga," he said, as if speaking of a childhood friend. "I read about it in the papers. Who put you onto me?"

"The old lady—her mother. She calls herself Mrs. Barton now and lives with some old geezer on the Contra Costa Canal. I ran into her today at Tina's funeral. She'd copped a couple of the letters you used to write Tina and had them stored away."

"How much did you give her for my name?"

"Nothing."

"That doesn't figure," he said, "but then maybe she's changed. When I first met Maggie she'd have taken your shirt and tried to sell you back the buttons."

"She's a little mellower now," I said, "but not much. I had to apply a little pressure."

"Cutting up old acquaintances is fun," he said, with his fingers gently drumming on his book, "but what do you want from me?"

"I don't know," I admitted. "Maybe..."

"Maybe nothing," he said. "I haven't seen Olga to talk to for at least eleven years, and I've been here for nearly six. I knew she'd changed her name, got her tits done, and was go-go dancing, but that's all. You know more about her than I do. I could tell you about the Olga Dombrowitz of sixteen or seventeen years ago—if I wanted to—but Tina D'Oro I know nothing about. I—"

There was a sharp, just-for-the-hell-of-it knock on his door, and a big, dun-haired nurse barged into Scarezza's room dragging a wheeled cart loaded with glasses and aluminum jugs. She had a face full of misdirected energy and cat's-eye glasses, which made her look slightly satanic.

"Evening, Antonio," she said briskly. "What'll it be: hot milk, cocoa, or Ovaltine? If you're a good boy, I could let you have some decaffeinated coffee."

I could tell from Scarezza's face that his idea of being a

good boy would be to tap dance on her windpipe, but she hovered blithely over the pre-sleep drinks like a magician about to produce a pink rabbit.

"Hot milk," said Scarezza in the voice of someone dealing with a natural enemy. "Two hot milks. Put the other one on my bill."

"Oooh, big spender," she said with the mocking good humor of someone who doesn't know she's hated. She poured out two tall glasses of steaming milk and put them on a small round table at the side of Scarezza's chair. "Well, ta, then, Antonio," she said cheerfully, bumping the cart out of his door into the hallway. "Sweet dreams!" The door closed behind her.

"Sometimes I think that's why I don't sleep," Scarezza said, "because she says 'sweet dreams' every night." He reached down beside the overstuffed cushion of his chair and came up with a flat, heavily embossed pint bottle of expensive Scotch whiskey. He poured a nice amount into each of the milk glasses and handed one to me.

"Here's to a painful death for Mrs. Monahan," he said, downing half of his milk and whiskey. I sipped mine and found it was better than I'd expected.

"Where was I?" he asked, wiping away a slight mustache of milk from his clean-shaven upper lip.

"You don't know anything about Tina D'Oro," I said wearily, feeling the familiar energy drain of wasting time and effort.

"That's right," Scarezza said with geriatric self-right-eousness. "I don't." He drank most of the other half of his milk and relaxed a bit. His grooved forehead smoothed out consider-ably, and his left hand lay at peace on his book. "I don't see how you could have expected me to," he added, "what with me not having seen her for so long."

"I didn't know that," I admitted. "When Maggie Barton told me about you and Tina and the kid, I just thought—"

"Kid?" said Scarezza, his brow furrowing again and looking at me as if I'd started speaking Urdu.

I opened my mouth to say something, but the word suddenly sank in. "Kid!" said Scarezza, coming out of his chair on a spring and throwing the rest of his milk all over my pant legs and shoes. "What kid? What kid is that?" The contortions of his old face somehow made him look younger. Or maybe it was the surge of adrenaline.

"Olga's baby," I said with that dumb feeling you get from telling somebody something he already knows. "Maggie said she came back from San Francisco a couple of years after she left home to have a baby and then went back to the city, leaving it with her mother. Hell, you ought to know that."

Scarezza didn't even hear that last bit. He was still standing, so I got to my feet. I can't bear people standing over me, not even sawed-off retired gangsters.

"Tell me about the baby," he demanded. "That was my baby. Olga never told me, the dirty bitch. Tell me, you punk!"

"There's not much to tell. The next winter after Tina left the baby with Maggie it died—probably of gastroenteritis. Maggie said she buried it in West Pittsburg."

I think maybe he was going to jump me, or at least that's what the remnants of his reflexes told him he ought to do. But this last one stopped him like a bullet in the chest.

"Died?" he said, but I knew he wasn't really asking me a question, so I stayed mum. It was his scenery; let him chew it up. His dry lips played silently with the word. I looked away. "Died," he said again to himself. But then he shot me an accusing look. "Was it a boy?"

"I don't know. Maggie didn't say." He made me feel stupid.

"Didn't say," he shouted. "Didn't say. She didn't say. You

dumb, crummy bastard. My son is dead, and you don't know anything about it. You probably don't even know if he was baptized, you son of a bitch."

"No," I said, "I don't." This wasn't fair; Scarezza was getting all the best lines. Scarezza was still standing in front of his chair, twitching in all directions as if warming up to do something rash. He'd jettisoned his glass somewhere.

Then he was moving toward a tall wardrobe against the wall at the foot of his bed. I'm glad nobody gave me the job of stopping him. Flinging the door open, he threw a suit of clothes on the unmade bed and began ripping off his robe and pajamas. He was mumbling to himself, probably cursing me and Maggie and Tina and anybody else handy. I stood and watched. Scarezza didn't even know I was there. Half dressed, he looked like a poorly fed turkey with a thin chest and saggy, blotchy skin. But as he tore off his pajama bottoms and donned a suit—a midnight-blue pinstripe number with a sixties cut—a new Scarezza appeared.

He didn't quite fill the suit anymore—his thin neck bobbled around in the starched collar of a white-on-white shirt—but I could see that he had once filled it well. There was nothing comical about him even now. He exchanged soft carpet slippers for a hard-looking pair of black wing tips and fumbled a bit with the laces before he got them knotted. The final touch was a snappy, narrow-brimmed Stetson with a chicken feather in the band. He looked ready for anything.

But he wasn't quite. Pausing to give a button on the wall next to his bed three sharp jabs, he plunged toward the desk behind me. I nimbly got out of his way and turned to watch him unlock and then open the long middle drawer of the desk. A thick sheaf of currency disappeared into an inside pocket of his suit coat, and his hand went back into the drawer. It came out full of black automatic, a matte-finished .45 with a muzzle that looked big enough to take a potted plant. He rammed a clip full of fat, ugly bullets into the butt of the automatic and clicked the safety back and forth a couple of times.

"Do you think you're going to need that?" I asked him.

Scarezza started and swiveled toward me with a surprised expression, pointing the pistol in my general direction. He'd forgotten that I was there.

"I might," he said levelly, looking me in the eye as if to head off objections. "You wouldn't be planning to try to stop me, would you?"

I started to explain that I wouldn't stand in his way even if he was off to rob a train, but the door came open in a hurry, and Thompson, textbook still in his hand, lurched in and stood with his mouth open, staring at the new Tony Scarezza.

"Mr. Scarezza!" he said.

"Thompson," said the old man, totally in command of the situation, "how much is that old heap of yours worth?"

"Heap?" asked Thompson. He wasn't getting many good lines either.

"Your car," said Scarezza snappily, "that thing that belches and farts every morning when you leave here. How much, boy?"

"My car? I don't know. Maybe a hundred dollars. Why—"

"Here's two hundred," said Scarezza, riffling through his wad of notes and shoving a few into the student's hand. "Give me your keys. Now!"

The confused Thompson, money still in one hand, dropped his book and dug for the car keys with the other. Scarezza snatched them, favored me with a crisp look and went through the doorway into the long hall. Thompson and I looked at each other for a moment and then followed him.

Scarezza was making good time down the polished hall and was nearly to the big double doors at the end of the ward when we caught sight of him. The sleep talker was again giving Madeline good, sound parental advice when we passed his door. On the marble apron at the top of the stairs a couple of nurses and a sleepy porter stood dopily watching Scarezza as he started down the spiral staircase. He'd had the good sense to put the automatic away. We followed him down like two store dicks after a fleeing shoplifter, and on about the second turn we all met Dr. Chapel coming up with an alert expression on his pleasant face. He looked as though he were either going to shake hands with the old man or tackle him.

He did neither. Instead, he looked past Scarezza at me and said disapprovingly, and I thought a bit disappointedly, "Mr. Goodey, I really cannot allow you to take a patient from this establishment without the proper procedure."

By this time he and Scarezza had passed each other without so much as a how-dee-do, and Chapel joined our merry little group in pursuit—although not very hot—of the old man.

"I'm not, Doctor," I told him as he fell into step between me and Thompson, who had given way eagerly. "Mr. Scarezza seems to be going someplace, and we're just following along. Would you care to join the posse?"

We were now in the foyer, and Scarezza was just going through the outer door. He went down the steps, but we stopped at the top and watched his dark figure leave the circle of light created by the tall street lamp.

"He seems determined to leave," I observed to Chapel. "Do you want me to stop him?" It was the least I could offer, considering that I'd set Scarezza in motion.

Chapel thought for a moment, but his forehead didn't show it. "No," he said in a long-drawn-out syllable, "we have no right to stop him. Mr. Scarezza is free to go where he likes."

From somewhere out in the dark we heard the wheezing roar of an old car coming reluctantly to life. Gears clashed, followed by a short screech of tires. Well, so long, Tony, I said to myself. Nice knowing you. But then, still with no lights on, a dusty 1957 Ford hardtop came barreling into the building's half-moon drive. Welcome back, Tony.

Scarezza brought the car to a sliding stop, leaned over, rolled down the passenger side window and shouted, "Hey, Goodey." Ever helpful, I trotted down the steps and leaned toward the window of the car.

"Yes, Mr. Scarezza?"

"Where exactly did you say Maggie was living on the Contra Costa Canal?"

"I didn't," I said, smiling in an effort to keep from seeming rude.

Mr. Scarezza said something in Italian and popped the clutch, nearly taking my head off as I stepped smartly out of the way. The car veered away into the second half of the horseshoe, and the headlights came on as it disappeared on a sharp turn to the right

By this time, Chapel had joined me on the narrow sidewalk. Thompson was on his way back to his anatomy textbook. The doctor seemed subdued and didn't say anything for a minute. Then he did.

"Mr. Goodey," he said with quiet wonder, "whatever did you say to Mr. Scarezza to get him to take off like that?"

"This is going to sound a bit strange, Doctor," I said, "but all I did was tell him that he's a father."

I know an exit line when I deliver one, so I walked over to my car, leaving Dr. Chapel to deal with his gaping jaw and fevered imagination.

17

As I drove back toward North Beach, I gave some passing thought to Scarezza and his .45 coming up against Jim Barton's old hawg-leg, but I didn't worry about it too much. They were both old enough to take care of themselves.

Broadway was alive. Bumper-to-bumper carloads of yokels stared at heel-to-toe pedestrians, who stared right back when they weren't trying to catch a free glimpse of flesh throughout the curtained entrances of topless clubs. They were all having a hell of a good time. The only person I could see having a better one was a heavy from the Klondike Klub who was carefully beating up a citizen who'd had the temerity to get drunk before ten p.m. And not at the Klondike. No sense of protocol.

The Broadway clubs were just getting into top gear. The quality trade was lined up across the sidewalk to get into a famous drag cabaret, and doorway barkers were frantically trying to skim off whatever cream was left. "Come on, come on," chanted a slick young thug in the doorway of Skin Alley, "come right in. Show's just starting this minute, folks. Step right in for a full hour of solid sensation, sizzling syncopation, and sex, sex, sex!" What the barker meant was a twenty-minute wait, thirty-five minutes of tantalization, five minutes of sock-it-to-'em, and out the suckers came, at least eight bucks poorer and very little wiser.

At a momentary break in the traffic, I cut off Broadway into a dimly lit network of small streets and alleyways, the part of North Beach few of the Saturday night crowd ever saw. When you live in North Beach you know all about these narrow, wandering streets and cul-de-sacs that offer parking places unblemished by tourists. I found these all full of tourists' cars, so I left the Morris half on the sidewalk and half in somebody's prize bed of daffodils. It was a short walk through a couple of alleys to The Jungle, where Irma was supposed to meet me.

I like alleys. You can never tell what you'll find in them. This one was full of surprises. At a point where one alley jogged slightly into another, I heard a sound somewhere in the darkness to the left of me. It was high-pitched, could have been a moan or a cry for help. It could have been a cocker spaniel in heat. Whatever it was, it stopped me and turned me two or three steps toward the sound. Where I stood was slightly lit by the dirty glow of a street light, but straight ahead of me was as flat and black as a strip of new blacktop road.

Out of that blackness a pair of strong hands grabbed the lapels of my jacket and jerked me forward. A foot in my stomach provided a nice amount of leverage, and I found myself flying through the darkness like an oversized bullet. Someone had been practicing his judo.

Fortunately, someone—small and hard, mind you, but better than nothing—got between me and the ground, so I slid off him to a fairly safe landing except for a dull pain in my knee, a scraped cheek, and a mouthful of something gritty and nasty. Not that I had a lot of time to feel thankful, because what felt like several dozen pairs of invisible hands began trying to grasp

each other—through my body. I lashed out with a foot hope-
fully, but hit nothing. And to make it worse, a pair of hands
latched onto my ankle and began dragging me on my back away
from the dimly lit alley into ultimate darkness. At the same
time, several pairs of well-shod feet began trying to make field
goals with my head. One glanced off a bit too sharply, taking, I
felt sure, one of my ears with it.

I thought about my police special tucked neatly among my
underwear in the trunk of my car two blocks away. More to the
point, I thought about the palm sap nestling next to the handkerchief in my left rear pocket. The palm sap is not necessarily
a very sporting weapon—six ounces of birdshot nicely wrapped
in a leather cover just made to fit in the palm with a couple of
loops for fingers—but it is comforting. To the sapper, that is. It
turns what looks like a lazy slap of the open hand into a real
knee trembler. The civil liberties people call it dirty pool, but
where were they now?

I lay there bumping feet first down the alley, protecting my
head with my arms as best I could and thinking that no trip
lasts forever. He had to drop my feet sometime. But I wasn't
sure that I was looking forward to that event. The outsides of
my arms and elbows were catching hell, not to mention my ribs.
After this, I could no longer claim a perfect body. My coat and
shirt were now knotted up under my arms, and bits of broken
glass and dog bones joined in the fun by scarifying my back
from waist to armpits. This was getting past a joke.

Then it happened. The fiend hauling on my ankles tripped
and fell backward. When my heels hit the ground, I gave up
self-defense for a moment, got my feet under me at the cost of a
nasty kick to the jaw, and sprang forward as far as I could,
hoping to come down on the dragger. At the same time I
reached back for the palm sap and slipped it on my right hand.
I came down with a satisfying crunch on a limb belonging to

the man on the ground and was rewarded with his howl of pain. Things were looking up, but I was still surrounded by slugging midgets.

An old vice-squadder once told me that in a fight a wall to your back was worth more than a ten-lesson course in jujitsu. His face had looked like a pound and a half of chopped liver, but I took his advice. Figuring that there had to be a wall to one side or the other, I flailed out with the sap and bulled my way to the left, knocking shadowy figures and trash cans out of my way as I went. My outstretched hand touched a brick wall, and I flung myself toward it. A bit too enthusiastically. My head hit the bricks with a jarring crunch and a pain which obscured everything but a solid thump to the kidney that one of my friends dealt me.

Shaking my head to clear it, I felt better and continued to hit anything I could see that would stand still. I was beginning to make out my attackers pretty well. There were five or six of them, none taller than my shoulder and all wearing some sort of wool skiing mask that seemed to take some of the sting out of my sap. They went down, all right, but they came bouncing right back up with hard knuckles and knees. None of them said a word; the only sounds were grunts and exploded breath and punches landing.

Don't let movie fights fool you. Throwing punches may be satisfying—if they land—but it's hard work. Every punch I gave took a little more out of me, and every one I took hurt a little more.

You'd think that at a time like that I'd be too busy to do much gazing around, but I began to notice something tall and bulky out in the alleyway at the entrance to our little arena. It had two legs and stood with hands on its hips. My first emotion was relief. Good deal. The Seventh Fleet was about to arrive and rescue me. But the figure didn't move. For what seemed like five minutes but may have been thirty seconds, it just stood there looking on. Well, I rationalized, as I discouraged a knee to the balls, it's no good rushing in if you can't see. He's acclimatizing his eyes to the darkness. Relief is only seconds away. But still he didn't move. One hand moved up to his mouth with a red point of light in it.

Of course, he was finishing off the last few drags on a cigarette. No use in being wasteful. But even when the cigarette had been shot pinwheeling against a wall, my rescuer didn't move. Maybe he was working out a game plan. It occurred to me with a sick feeling that maybe he was one of them. But just then I had to devote my attention to one little monkey who was trying to chew off my thumb while another of them jumped on my back and a third party took my legs out from under me, dropping me into a heap of rotting vegetables. One arm was pinned under me, and somebody was trying to rip the other one off.

I was just about to swallow my manly pride and start crying for help when my arm was suddenly freed, and the lad who had been wrenching it flew backward over a row of vegetable boxes. Someone was among the enemy, dealing out vicious and efficient punches, and quite quickly my attackers began to lose heart. Somehow, as he threw them away, they didn't come back, but melted into the darkness. And without even saying goodbye. Soon I felt a pair of large hands grab the tattered front of my jacket and pull me to my feet.

"Things were beginning to look a bit dark for you, pal," my rescuer said. Then he recognized me—or pretended to. "Goodey!" said Bruno Kolchik.

I didn't say anything. I was too busy taking a rough inventory of my parts and accessories. I seemed to be in one piece, if you don't include extraneous bits of skin I couldn't account for. My clothing—never much to start with—had suffered. I was not a well-dressed private detective. However, my palm sap was virtually unblemished, and I put it away tenderly. A boy's best friend is not his mother.

All this time Bruno was watching me with an expression halfway between smug self-satisfaction and idle curiosity. I didn't like either much and thought about getting the palm sap out again. Then I thought about the way he'd handled my attackers. Instead, I did a good neat job of tucking in my shirt and smoothing down what was left of my jacket.

"It took you quite a while to pitch in," I said accusingly. "What were you waiting for—the first body count?" I was neither friendly nor grateful, which is perhaps a personal failing of mine.

"Hell, Goodey," he said good-naturedly, "how quick would you be to jump into a back-alley brawl in North Beach? I didn't have any idea it was you until I pulled you from the bottom of the heap." He had me there. If our positions had been reversed, I'd be two blocks away whistling, and he'd be getting his spleen ventilated. That is, if I could believe that he didn't know it was me. I had only his word for that.

"Anyway," he said, "you don't seem to have suffered any permanent damage. It's a good thing you were wearing your old clothes. Do you have any idea who your little friends were?"

"It could have been my fan club, but somehow I doubt it. None of them left a visiting card. But if you run into half a dozen bruised midgets, you might ask them a few questions."

"I'll do that," he said. "In the meantime, where were you going?"

"Why do you want to know?" I asked cautiously.

"You're a suspicious bastard, Goodey," he said.

"All right, I was going to The Jungle. Now what?"

"I'll walk along with you," Bruno said. "I might even buy you a drink, if you don't mind too much."

"Okay," I said grudgingly, and we started walking. Neither of us said anything. I was too busy trying to figure out his motivation for becoming my best buddy. Goodey's First Law is always mistrust someone in power who is being too obliging. I liked The Brother better when he was his own nasty self. I didn't know what Bruno was thinking, and that bothered me a bit, too.

Sherman, the night manager at The Jungle, nearly wet himself when he saw The Brother, and started herding us toward a star sucker table directly under the flying tits. But Bruno turned toward a back table in the dark and stared at two local bravos until they remembered that they had a date elsewhere. He waded toward the table, memorizing the clientele, but I headed for the Gents' room and a bit of general repairs.

I didn't look too bad in the cracked and cloudy men's-room mirror. A bit of soap and cold water took off a little more dirty skin, but I could have used some pancake on my scraped cheek. When I finished, I was sure that my mother could have picked me out of any Tenderloin lineup. I was rather hurt when a local queen with purple talons came in, caught my eye in a routine way and then shuddered delicately and ran out of the door.

As I came back into the main bar, I asked Sherman to watch for Irma Springler and tell her that I was there. He promised insincerely, and I set out for Bruno's table, where he sat in lonely splendor like a leper at a convention of hypochondriacs. He didn't seem to mind a bit. Bruno waved me to a chair and pointed out the drink he'd bought me. Or rather, the free drink the management had given him for me. Bruno's money was no good at The Jungle, strangely enough.

I sipped my drink. It didn't seem to be poisoned. I relaxed as much as aching muscles and increasing paranoia would allow.

Bruno surveyed the crowd at The Jungle as if about to

order a mass arrest. Finally he spoke. "Is it too much to ask, Goodey, whether you've made any progress on the job we gave you?" A fair question, I figured, considering the job and Bruno's connection with the mayor.

"I can tell you one thing," I said. "I've eliminated a number of very remote suspects. That leaves a couple of million to go, but I'm working on it."

Bruno just looked tired. "Is it possible, Goodey," he asked, "that we made a mistake bringing you back?"

"Maybe," I said, "but then it's possible that I'm telling you less than I know. Just possible."

His face said he didn't believe it, but before he could expand on the theme, I became aware of someone standing next to our table. It was Irma Springler.

The Brother's heavy eyes lit up at the sight of a pretty girl. At that moment, The Jungle was between shows, and its tacky stage yawned emptily in the shower of cold light. It was obvious that Irma hadn't noticed The Brother sitting with me and certainly hadn't expected to be sharing a table with him. Unless Bruno was a great actor, he didn't have the slightest idea who she was.

I thought for a moment that Irma was going to bolt, but then she got a grip on herself and sat down in a chair by my side as far as possible from Bruno. All the while I kept smiling like a sex maniac. Sherman suddenly appeared with a drink for Irma and seemed disposed to hang around and chat. My fear was that he'd inadvertently drop her first name. Bruno was not that much of a dope; he'd know the second name.

"That's *fine*, just *fine*, Sherman," I said in my best Gauleiter voice. "We'll call you if we need you." Sherman started and then shied off like a big dog accustomed to rebuffs but always hoping for better.

That left the three of us. Bruno was looking interested in

Irma and rather pleased with himself. Irma looked as though she didn't know whether to flee or go for his face with a broken bottle. I don't know how I looked, but all I wanted to do was keep Irma out of official hands. I knew Johnny Maher was looking for her; Bruno probably knew the same.

"Say," I said stupidly, "you two probably don't know each other." Boring hard into Irma's eyes with mine, I said, "Alice, this is Deputy Chief of Police Kolchik." I couldn't have been more emphatic if I'd gotten up on the table and tap-danced his title in Morse code. "Chief, this is Alice Parsons, a friend of mine." I only hoped she wouldn't forget the name.

"How do you do, Alice?" said Bruno with a heavy bonhomie of someone who is sure he's going to be liked. "Joe didn't tell me he was going to meet someone as pretty as you here." Oh, me and Bruno were great buddies, we were.

"And I didn't expect him to show up with a copper, Mr. Kolchik," Irma said. "I don't like coppers." She didn't say it quietly, and we were suddenly in the middle of a growing island of silence. Oh, great, a cop hater. Just what the situation called for.

Bruno leaned back in his chair with the expression of a man who'd just been hit in the face with a strawberry waffle: not hurt, but puzzled and just beginning to get sore. Irma didn't give him a chance. "It's not just that you're a copper," she said in a voice diamond-edged with malice. "Some of them are honest. But you're a political cop. You got where you are on your brother's back. Don't think I don't know who you are."

The famous Kolchik ears were turning a translucent carmine. Bruno put both big paws on the table as if ready to vault over it and gritted through his large teeth: "Listen, *miss*"— he said the word the way anyone else would have used *slut*— "you may know who I am, but I'd like to know just who the hell you think you are. Who are you, anyway?"

I honestly think she was going to tell him, but just then, in the smoky middle distance, I spotted Phil Franks coming our way. It would be more accurate to say that he was drifting our way like a giant barge cut loose in a choppy sea, with the hapless Sherman acting as guide-cum-scout, apologizing for upset drinks and customers accidentally pushed under tables. Phil announced his impending presence and saved Irma's bacon by croaking out: "Good evening, Bruno, welcome to The Jungle." Phil's not shy.

This cut short both Irma's answer and The Brother's likely reaction. Quickly becoming aware that he'd soon be sharing a table with me, Phil—not Bruno's favorite person—and a hostile broad, Kolchik knew a losing combination when he saw one and looked for a way out. Not seeing one, he decided to make one. Pausing only to glower at me in a very meaningful way, Bruno headed for the other exit with little regard for the paying customers he trampled.

"Hey," said one of these socialites in the middle of the mob, "who do you think you're shoving around?" He struggled to his feet.

"You, Buster," said The Brother, putting the citizen back in a sitting position so forcefully that the chair splintered under him. Another job of soothing for Sherman.

Irma and I had plenty of time to hiss at each other before Fat Phil arrived.

"What the hell," I said. "Here I am trying to keep you out of the hands of the police, and you practically stick your head in Kolchik's mouth. What gives?"

"I've got my reasons," she said sulkily. "I can't stand that bastard. Besides, nobody asked you to save me from anything. I can take care of myself. I was just about to tell your big buddy who I was anyway."

Any clever answers I might have had were stifled by the

arrival of Fat Phil. I gave Irma an I'll-sort-you-out-later look and turned toward Phil.

He slipped into two chairs as close to the table as he could manage and sat glistening with sweat and looking like a text-book case of cardiac arrest. Sherman appeared with more drinks for us and Phil's sickly special. Somehow Phil got the glass to his lips a few times, and his green complexion turned several shades lighter.

"So you found her," he finally gasped, favoring Irma with a proprietary leer. "What do you think?"

"Sensational, Phil," I said. "You'll make another million, at least. Your Doc Irving is quite a little miracle worker."

He frowned. Phil didn't like his little secrets discovered. But then he shrugged, a massive operation in itself, and turned to Irma. "How did you make out with our friend today?" he asked.

"All right," said Irma in a carefully controlled voice, keeping it businesslike and cool. "He's ready to start Monday morning."

"How about you?" he asked slyly, looking intently into her face. "Are you ready? Are you sure you're ready?"

I was watching Irma's face, too, and she handled it beauti-fully. "I'm ready, Phil," she said without a tremor of revulsion and without coyness either, "or I wouldn't have gone to see Dr. Irving today." She held his eye, not consciously or challeng-ingly, but definitely, until he shifted back to me, apparently satisfied. I'd have to watch that girl. I was no match for her.

"You see, Joe," he said, "she's going to be sensational. Would you believe she's only twenty-one years old?"

"No."

"Thousands will," he said with self-satisfaction. "Thou-sands will. And I've got her on an ironclad contract."

All three of us knew exactly what he was talking about, but

none of us said it. And each had a different motive for saying nothing. The ghost of Tina D'Oro sat in the empty chair at the table.

"Only one big problem, Joe," Phil rumbled on. "I still haven't got the right name for Irma to use. Can you think of a good one?" I could have made some interesting suggestions. But I had to watch my smart mouth and Irma's tender sensibilities if she was going to be any help at all. So I just turned my mouth up at the corners in what might have passed for a smile.

"Sorry, Phil," I said. "I'm not much good on the creative side, but if it will help, I'll give it a lot of thought."

I'm sure he was about to thank me profusely when the lights dimmed and the house band began to thrash about in the pit, making noises. But, instead of one of the second-line bimbos coming on, a large motion-picture screen began to descend in the jungle-clearing stage. And Sherman's anonymous voice said, "And now, friends and gentle customers, as we promised you, The Jungle proudly presents, in living color, in brilliant detail, the one, the only, the *Late Great Tina D'Oro!*"

The pit band went mad on cue, and I could see Irma instantly go tense. She still had a glass in her hand, and it looked as though she was going to crush it. Her teeth went into her full lower lip, and I knew she wasn't going to sit through any Tina films. I put a restraining, and I hoped soothing, hand on her wrist and started to my feet. Phil's eyes were on the screen. His face had taken on an abstract, distant look.

"Sorry, Phil," I said, pulling Irma woodenly to her feet, "we've got a hot date on the other side of town."

"Sure, Joe," he said absently. "See you later."

I started moving Irma away from him as fast as I could, but I heard his fat voice following me: "Take good care of the merchandise, Joe." I don't think Irma heard, and I pretended that I didn't.

Moving Irma through the tightly bunched tables was not easy. My already aching arms were starting to crumble by the time we reached the side door. But outside on the sidewalk, Irma took several long gulps of cool night air and seemed to recover. She moved slightly away from me and supported herself with a hand on a brick wall.

"Thanks," she said after a moment "I didn't know what to do in there." She shook her head and shuddered deeply at the memory.

"Are you okay now?"

"I think so."

"What now?" I said.

"Now, I'm going home," she answered. She took a couple of steps as if to demonstrate that she could walk, but then her legs gave way a bit, and she leaned back against the wall. "It has been a hard day," she said.

"I've got a car a couple of blocks away," I said. "If you could hold that wall up for five minutes, I'll bring it here and give you a ride home."

She looked back toward the side entrance of The Jungle and then at the stream of humanity bobbing and throbbing along Broadway. "I'd rather walk with you to the car," she said. "I don't think I could stand five more minutes of this particular location."

I thought about the most direct route to the Morris, and then about the banditos I might run into on it. It wouldn't do to meet them again so soon with a slightly woozy girl in tow. That is, unless she carried a palm sap, too. I decided to give that route a pass until I was a bit better prepared. We'd take a longer, safer way.

"All right," I said, "but we'll have to walk along Broadway for a bit. Here, let me give you a bit of support." I put an arm around her waist—a very nice waist with just the right amount of flesh on it—and pulled her away from the wall. I could feel her resist at first, then give up and put her arm around my waist.

We must have seemed like any other happy Saturday night couple, except that one of us looked as if he'd been rolled around in the gutter by a pack of Great Danes. Irma had so far been polite enough not to mention it. Or maybe she hadn't noticed.

We had only half a block of Broadway to negotiate and made it unscathed. A picket line of young sailors at one point offered to block the sidewalk. But at the last moment they broke up in a welter of sub-drunken giggles and shy looks at Irma. Then we turned off into the small but well-lit street which would lead to the cul-de-sac where the Morris lurked. Nothing jumped out of the shadows at us.

The short drive to the 400 block of Union Street was uneventful. Irma was slumped against the passenger-side door, saying nothing, and I was beginning to feel every bruised and aching muscle, sinew and bone. I leaned the car against a curb in front of her building, flicked the ignition off and went limp. Nobody said anything.

After a decent interval, I said, "Let's flip a coin to see who carries whom up the stairs."

"I've a better idea," Irma said, and her voice sounded much more relaxed. "I'll just sleep here in the car. You won't mind, will you?"

"Not if you'll let me wash up and change clothes up at your place. In case you didn't notice, I'm less than my impeccable self this evening."

"I did notice," she said, "but I didn't like to say anything. What happened? Did that appointment turn nasty?"

"Not exactly. But on the way to meet you at The Jungle I took a shortcut through an alley and met a group of gentlemen who took a dislike to me and weren't shy in letting me know."

"I hope you weren't badly hurt."

"We won't know until the post-mortem," I said. "Do you think we're ready to attempt the climb to your place yet?"

"No, but if we don't go now, I'll never get up the nerve again." Getting one of my suitcases out of the trunk of the car, I tried to remember exactly when I had put it there. It seemed a long, long time ago.

The stairs up to Irma's apartment hadn't gotten any less steep, and the suitcase on my arm seemed to be doubling in weight at every floor. But finally we were standing in front of Irma's door. Nanny Goat next door stuck her head out, took one look at me and my suitcase, snorted sharply, and ducked back in with a slam of the door.

"There goes your reputation in the neighborhood," I said.

"It couldn't be any lower with her," said Irma, unlocking the door and stepping inside. "She's convinced that I'm a prostitute, and when I'm out she slips little notes under my door in favor of chastity and against the sins of the flesh. The bathroom is straight through that door on the right. Help yourself."

I marched, suitcase in hand, toward the bathroom door. Irma's apartment was almost military in its simplicity. The walls that weren't painted a flat white were covered with cork or hessian. Paintings or other decorations were few. Bric-a-brac was nonexistent. The couch was a flat slab of foam rubber scattered with a few cushions. A door led to a small kitchen, and beyond that another probably opened onto her bedroom. The apartment wasn't quite so anonymous as mine, but if it was stamped with a personality, it was a subtle one.

In the bathroom—shower, no bathtub—I stripped off my tatters and admired myself in a long, narrow mirror. I looked like an aerial map of a long, thin peninsula with the elevations marked out in bruises, some blue, some faint mauve. My days as a figure model were over. In the shower, the pins and needles of the hot spray went to work like Torquemada's stiletto. I wished I'd stayed dirty. But soon the heat began to wash away some of the pain, and I started to feel faintly human again. As I dressed, I debated whether to strap my pistol on again, but decided against it. I left it on top of the clothes in my suitcase, but loaded it just in case.

When I got back out into the living room, Irma had two drinks poured and was sitting on the foam-rubber sofa. She looked fully recovered. She looked better than that. In a relaxed state her face was more than pretty. Doc Irving would have been happy to claim her short, straight nose as his own work. I sipped my drink and enjoyed looking at her.

"Do you always carry suitcases of clothes around in the trunk of your car?" Irma asked.

"Not really," I told her, explaining as vaguely as possible that through no fault of my own my apartment was full of Chinese delinquents and, possibly, cops. In theory, I said, I had a bed there. But the odds against finding it empty were less than encouraging. I may have said this with a slight ulterior motive, sitting as we were on a couch which looked comfortable enough to sleep on.

Irma's reaction was mixed. She didn't laugh in my face, but neither did she melt with sympathy and offer me a place to sleep, although I didn't give up hoping. For the moment, though, I thought I'd better steer the conversation back into a channel which might lead in the direction of Tina's murderer. Unless, of course, I was having drinks with her right now. I tried to bear that in mind.

"If it won't upset you," I said, "could we talk a bit more about the last time you saw Tina and the events leading up to the night you found her—uh—found her in her apartment?"

"I suppose we'd better," she said. She looked me dead in the eye. "I want to find out who killed Tina as much as you do, Joe. Maybe more than you do. To you, it's just a job. Am I right?"

"Yes," I said. Aside from threats coming from various Kolchiks and their minions, it was just a job. This was a girl you couldn't bullshit. It made life easier if I didn't try.

"Well, to me it's the most important thing in my life. I hate the whole idea, but if I have to, I'll let Dr. Irving inflate my breasts like footballs. And I'll shake them at anybody who comes into The Jungle if it will get me closer to knowing who killed Tina."

"And what if whoever did it has nothing to do with The Jungle? What if it was somebody completely outside North Beach, someone who'll never come into the club again?"

"Then I'll have been shaking my tits in vain, won't I? That's the chance I've got to take. But I have a feeling that I'm not wasting my time. Tina's world was a small one. She'd never lived any place but North Beach since she came here. I could count on the fingers of one hand the people she knew from more than five miles away from The Jungle."

"That narrows it down considerably," I said. "But let's try to thin the suspects a bit more. For instance, who's your current favorite?" She didn't answer right away, and it wasn't because she was considering the question. Something clouded behind those blue-gray eyes. Little Irma wasn't being completely candid with her new partner in crime detection.

"Let's not kid each other, Irma," I said. "You've got a favorite, but you're not going to tell me who it is. Right?" She did it again—looked me in the eye. A disconcerting habit for a pretty girl.

"You're right, Joe. I have. Are you telling me everything you know?"

She had me there.

"All right," I said. "Every partnership has its little running-in difficulties. Let's just agree not to lie to each other. That will help. If you want to keep something to yourself, that's okay by me. And I'll do the same. Now, just for the hell of it, run once more through the last time you saw Tina."

Patiently, Irma recounted that last meeting with Tina, the setting of Tina's hair, what they said, as best she could recall, the parting after making a date for early the next morning after the last show at The Jungle. Then she switched to when she found Tina's body. Nothing new there, either, until she was telling me, quite calmly, I thought, about the chaos that set in after the door to the apartment had been opened. Then something occurred to her.

"Joe," she said, "I can't put my finger on it, but even at a time like that—with Tina dead on the floor—I found myself looking around the apartment, just aimlessly gazing. Maybe to avoid looking at Tina. They tried to get me out of the apartment, but I wouldn't go. I kept thinking—it's the strangest thing—I kept thinking something was missing. Something I was used to seeing just wasn't there. Maybe it's my imagination, but it's driving me crazy. I can't think what it was." She put long, slim fingers to either side of her forehead.

"Don't strain," I said. "It'll come to you when you least expect it. The harder you try, the more elusive it will be. Let me take your mind off it for a minute with another question."

She looked up at me under heavy lashes with a look I couldn't consider completely trusting. Or maybe it was just wariness. "What is it?"

"Why did you have a go at Bruno Kolchik tonight?"

"I don't like him."

"That was obvious," I said. "But you must have some reason. It's not just because he's a cop. Or even because he got to the top on his brother's back. There's got to be another reason."

"Does there?"

"Yes. Remember our no-lies policy. How can I trust you if you so obviously don't trust me?"

She thought this over carefully. If I say so myself, it had the ring of truth. Finally, she said: "All right, I'll give it a try. I went for Bruno Kolchik because of something Tina told me." She stopped as if reconsidering her candor.

"And what was that?" I prompted.

"A couple of weeks ago, Bruno came to see Tina and told her that the mayor was about to get rid of her. For political reasons or something. What's more, he suggested that it might be a good idea if he—Bruno—sort of took the mayor's place."

"And what did Tina say?"

"She told him to fuck off, of course," Irma said positively. "And when he hinted that she might get leaned on, Tina offered to claw his rotten eyes out."

"She told you this?" I asked.

"Of course."

"And do you think she told the mayor about it?"

Irma bit a thumbnail. "I don't know. Maybe she didn't get a chance to. Tina wasn't one to rush into something without thinking it over."

Bruno's little try at Tina gave me something to think over. Maybe he would bear looking into. I copped a look at my watch. It was past midnight, and my body felt like four in the morning. I drained the watery liquid in the bottom of my glass and stood up.

"I'd better hit the road for home," I said mock-heroically. "The later I stay out, the more diminutive Chinese I'll have to evict from my bed. It's not all fun being a private detective." I looked around for my suitcase, knowing very well where it was.

Finally spotting it and limping—genuinely—over to it, I picked the case up as if it weighed several tons and turned bleakly toward the door.

"Thanks very much," I said, "for the use of your bathroom. I leave here a cleaner if not a wiser man. If you need to find me..." I saw that she was fighting a losing battle with a smile and let my voice trail off. I stood looking at her and trying not to appear too foolish. I don't think I was succeeding.

"If you'd like," she said fatalistically, "you could sleep on this couch. It's not very soft, but..."

"Great," I said, dropping my suitcase and no doubt half of the plaster on the ceiling of the apartment below. "I accept." I never have been very good at mealy-mouthed if-it-won't-be-too-much-troubles. An expression flickered across her face. It could have been a second thought. Too late for that.

It didn't take Irma long to make up the couch into a neat little bed topped with a satin-edged blanket. We said our civil goodnights. The door to her bedroom had hardly closed when I stripped off all my clothes, hobbled to the couch and slipped between the smooth, cool sheets. I lay there trying not to think about who killed Tina and attempting to ignore the multitude of little pains gathering like the Cherokee nation to massacre my central nervous system.

I closed my eyes, and I could swear that my eyelids ached. I hoped that those lads from the alley were going to feel as bad in the morning as I did right then. I tried to imagine that a soothing, healing liquid was flowing over my body, but that hurt, too.

Sometime later, a noise, not much of a noise, more like a swish, jerked my eyelids open, and a small, painful turn of my head told me that I wasn't alone. Something pale, filmy and diaphanous was moving toward me from the direction of Irma's room. It was Irma. The light from a moth-splattered street lamp outside the window showed that she was barefoot and wearing a translucent, off-white nightgown which skimmed the top of her knees.

"Joe," she said. "Joe, are you still awake?"

"Yes, but I'm not so sure I'm still alive."

She was at the side of the couch, leaning, then kneeling.

"I can't sleep," she said. "Tina's in her grave, and I'm all alone. I don't think I can stand to be alone tonight. May I sleep with you, Joe?"

I won't go into all the thoughts that ricocheted through my head. They were too various and not all to my credit. But I knew what she meant. The night that Pat caught that final, irretrievable plane to New York I was reduced to sleeping with a big, plush teddy bear I'd bought her in happier days. It was better than nothing. I suppose, to Irma, so was I. I didn't really think it was love.

It won't do to hesitate too long in a situation like that. "Sure," I said. "But for God's sake be careful. Don't bump me too hard, or I'll probably come apart all over your couch."

"Don't move," she said softly. "I'll climb over you to the other side."

Something feather-soft fluttered over my face, leaving a suggestion of a dry, clean but faintly exotic perfume. That didn't hurt a bit. She lifted the covers slightly and then was between them, lying on her left side facing me. We weren't actually touching, but I could feel the slight pressure of her body on the bottom sheet.

"There," she said. "Did that hurt you?"

"No, but it's the only thing that's happened to me in the last few hours that hasn't." I could feel her breath softly on my right ear.

"Where does it hurt most?"

"Everywhere," I said. "I feel as though a vast herd of tiny

elephants has been using me for a parade ground. It would be easier for me to tell you where it hurt least."

"There?" she breathed, placing a warm hand on my bare chest.

"Nope," I said. "One of those little bastards was butting me. I think he was trying to put his head through my chest."

"How about there?"

She moved her hand down in easy stages over my ribs to my stomach, which when last seen had looked as if someone had painted a stormy sunset around my navel. My involuntary wince answered her question, and Irma's hand wandered slowly southward, then paused.

"Joe," she said with a note of genuine surprise in her voice, "aren't you wearing any clothes at all?"

"Nope," I said. "I wasn't expecting any company tonight."

"I wasn't expecting to offer any," she said. "But somehow it just..."

"Happened?"

"Yes. I got into bed and found that I couldn't help thinking about Tina. I didn't want to. I've been fighting it ever since... ever since Thursday night. But it caught up with me, and I just couldn't stand to be alone."

My ears were taking in what she was saying, but my mind couldn't stop thinking about her hand on my hipbone. Somewhere in back of my mind a spark of feeling was rising which had nothing to do with Tina or the hurt my body had received. I think Irma noticed. She moved her hand even farther down.

"Does it hurt there?"

"It does actually," I said. "One of my friends had a knee like a pile driver. But don't stop."

18

I woke up with the taste, smell, and feel of Irma stamped on my bruised senses, but no Irma. I was alone on the couch, Irma's nightgown was still on the floor, and the sound of the shower was coming out of the open bathroom door. I got up with a grunt of vividly remembered pain and walked stiffly into the bathroom. She was behind the opaque glass door, and steam was billowing out of the shower stall.

"Good morning," I called. "If you don't take all day in there, I'll buy you breakfast at Rico's."

Irma turned off the shower, slid the door open and came out wearing only a towel tied over her hair. When she saw me, she stopped and stared. "My God," she said, "you weren't kidding last night. You look terrible."

"Thanks," I said, wiping the long mirror with a hand towel and taking a look. There was a lot in what she said. Most of my bruises had turned a nasty yellow with red and blue overtones. They covered most of my body from knees to chest, with a few wild-card extras above and below. An especially vivid blotch over my left kidney made me wince just looking at it. But, except for general soreness, I didn't feel much worse than I used to after a fairly dirty football game. Maybe I would later.

Irma laid a hand softly on the least bruised part of my rib cage. It didn't hurt a bit. "I tried to tell you," I said, "but you wouldn't listen. I think you must have done most of this last night."

"Fool!" she said, kissing me and going out of the connecting door to her bedroom. If this was what a private detective's life was like, I was sorry I hadn't switched over years ago. Even with Maher and the midgets from the alley. By the time I showered again and shaved, Irma was dressed and waiting impatiently.

Rico's is one of those sidewalk cafes where a certain sort of San Franciscan likes to be seen eating overpriced bacon and eggs and reading the funny papers. If it's a good day with blue skies and that luminous sunshine only San Francisco gets, over-cooked eggs taste like ambrosia, and local eccentrics are transformed into wits. If not, you sit with your teeth chattering in the dirty wind, picking grit out of your food and watching people file toward the Golden Gate Bridge to commit suicide.

This Sunday morning was bright, if a little brisk, and I felt just fine sitting across the table from Irma and watching the clientele pickle their livers with Ramos gin fizzes. The feeling is that if it's frothy and sweet, it's not really alcohol. Rico must have been doing some sort of penance. He was out on the sidewalk taking orders himself, but in his usual half-hearted manner which said they might never get to the kitchen. He sneered when we turned down a pre-breakfast drink, took our orders and then lingered to enjoy the view down the front of Irma's long-sleeved white blouse.

"I know you're having a good time, Rico," I said, "but we're hungry. If you'll get me a telephone, I'll send out for a sandwich."

Rico knows who I am—vaguely—but pretends not to. He

looked past me with the distantly pained expression of someone who once watched his mother drown rather than ruin a new suit. Then he did a fairly military about-face and marched stiffly toward the kitchen.

"Do you really expect to get any food talking to him like that?" Irma asked me. "He's probably gone to get the bouncer. I've seen Rico refuse service to people just because he didn't like their posture."

"That's because they smiled at him instead of kicking his shins," I said. "If I'd set his coat on fire, we'd have our breakfast by now." Just then the double doors to the kitchen came flying open, and a giant in a dirty white coat came out carrying a huge tray high overhead on one arm. With five long strides, he was at our side, had commandeered a tray stand and was sliding covered dishes of food onto our table like a demon blackjack dealer.

Working as smoothly as the best shell-and-pea operator in the world, he quickly uncovered and re-covered each of the stainless- steel containers, giving us an intriguing glimpse of mushrooms, bacon, sausage, kippers, oatmeal, scrambled eggs, fried eggs, steak, and two or three other things I've forgotten. This was not the simple bacon, eggs and English muffins we'd ordered, and the hostile stares of six over-dressed tourists across the sidewalk gave me a good clue to its rightful owner.

"With the compliments of Monsieur Rico," said the magician, pouring two giant cups of coffee and vanishing into the kitchen.

"Will you have some scrambled eggs?" I asked Irma with an I-told-you-so look. We began to nibble around the edges of this feast. There was a momentary flurry as the robbed tourists leaped up from their chairs and flounced down the sidewalk, but then Rico's settled down to its usual quiet hum of dropped names and characters assassinated.

Something was still nagging Irma as she chewed thoughtfully on a bit of Rico's breakfast steak. Finally, she said: "You were wrong, Joe. It still hasn't come. I've been trying not to think about that thing—whatever it was—that was missing from Tina's apartment that night. But I can't help it. I've got to get back into that apartment and see if I can remember what it was. It may not be important, but I'll rest easier if I know."

"How are you going to manage that?" I asked, peering in at a flock of grilled kippers and deciding against it. "Fat Phil's not offering guided tours, is he?"

"Well, you're a policeman—you were a policeman. Can't you jimmy the door or something?"

That's the public for you, always giving a copper credit for useful skills and unethical methods. "I don't know," I said. "It's been a long time since I did any burglary, but I could have a go at it. I wouldn't mind taking a look at Tina's place myself. The scene of the crime and all that. But why don't we just ask Fat Phil and skip all the counterspy routine?"

"Do you think he'd let us?"

My educated guess was interrupted when Irma reached over and jogged my arm. "Joe," she said, "I think there's somebody across the street who's trying to get your attention."

I looked up, and there a couple of feet back in a tall, thin alley was Lee, one of Gabe Fong's juvenile delinquents. I knew him by the flashy club jacket. He was mouthing something fairly urgent, so I motioned for him to come over. We had plenty of breakfast left. But he took a backward step deeper into the alley and gestured even more frantically. If they went back to making silent movies, that boy's future was assured.

I thought about ignoring him, but then the better side of my nature prevailed, and I decided that I'd better at least find out what he wanted. Spearing a pork sausage and gulping some coffee, I stood up.

"I'll be right back," I told Irma. "Then we'll see what we can do about getting into Tina's apartment. This shouldn't take long." When I started across Broadway, Lee was no longer in sight, but I found him a few feet farther down the alley looking as agitated as a smooth-faced, nineteen-year-old Chinese boy can.

"Mr. Goodey," he said, "come with me quickly. Gabriel Fong is in trouble. Hurry!" He was already scuttling sideways down the alley, looking back anxiously at me like a relay runner waiting for the baton. Only I was the baton.

"Trouble?" I said wittily. "What sort of trouble?" I kept moving with Lee in order to keep him within earshot. Soon we were twenty yards or more inside the alley. "Stand still, damn it," I said. "What do you mean, Gabriel Fong is in trouble?"

Lee stopped and turned fully back toward me. "I can't tell you now," he said. "There's no time."

I reached out and grabbed his thin, bony arm between shoulder and elbow. I dug my heels in, and he had to stop or lose the arm. But he wasn't very happy about it. "There is time," I insisted. "Look, either you tell me what you're talking about, or I'm not going any place with you. Now, just what sort of trouble is Fong in?"

Lee's face underwent a disturbing transition. His arm stopped pulling against my grip, and he turned to face me. I automatically relaxed my hold on him.

"To tell the truth, Joe Goodey," he said, "Gabriel Fong isn't in trouble at all. But you are." His other hand came up fast with a white-metal .32 caliber revolver in it. It couldn't have cost more than ten bucks and looked about as dangerous as a cap pistol. All by itself, my hand let go of Lee's arm and started minding its own business.

I didn't bother going through the what's-the-meaning-of-this routine. I figured that if he wanted to tell me, he'd tell me.

My police special, which I'd finally gotten around to putting on my belt, hung there as useless as an extra kidney.

"The wall," said Lee, shoving his shiny toy gun up toward my sternum, too far away to grab but close enough to kill even if it merely exploded as he pulled the trigger. Up close, I could see that it was one of those Czechoslovakian imports that had been blowing hands off lately. I felt I ought to warn him, but somehow it didn't seem appropriate at that moment. "Put your hands against the wall wide apart, Goodey, and lean," he said.

I knew the drill. Lee had learned his lesson well from all those cop shows on TV. I leaned forward until my hands were touching the wall and only my toes were still on the ground. A deft hand plucked my pistol out of its holster, disappeared it and then delved into my left rear pocket for my palm sap. I had been hoping he wouldn't do that.

"Very nice," said Lee, admiring the sap.

"It'll do," I said. "How are you feeling this morning, Lee? A little stiff and bruised perhaps?"

I shouldn't have said that. Suddenly my feet were swept out from under me and I fell heavily against the wall, absorbing most of the fall with my cheek—the unscraped one. I felt the sting of the sap against the back of my head, not hard enough to stun me but enough to hurt like hell.

For some time I didn't say anything, just lay there in the dirt trying to hold the back of my head on and doing my best not to scream out with pain. I nearly bit my lower lip off and waited for the waves of stinging pain to recede a little. Finally they did, and I was left with a bleeding face, a stinking headache, and Lee standing there waiting for me to do something stupid. I didn't do it.

"Do you think I could get up now?" I asked through a dry and dusty mouth.

"Of course," said Lee, friendly enough, but he didn't lend

me a hand. When I got to my feet and turned around, he was standing a few feet away with the Czech special peeking coyly out of his club jacket. "We'd better hurry now, Goodey," he said. "Somebody wants to see you."

19

"Who might that be?" I asked Lee, well aware that he was walking behind me and just slightly to the left.

"You'll find out soon enough," Lee said, but he wasn't unfriendly. I liked that. It's bad enough being roughed up without having rudeness thrown in.

"Do you mind if I have a guess?"

"Go ahead," he said, "but just keep moving and don't try anything funny. My boss won't mind much if I leave you here dead instead of bringing you in."

He was lucky to have such a lenient employer. Some would be furious. The conclusion that his tolerant chief was my roommate, Gabriel Fong, forced itself upon me. That hurt. But we weren't going toward my apartment. My friend was prodding me through the back door to Chinatown, the drab and dreary side of the gaudy front that tourists think is the Chinese quarter of San Francisco. It was a nice morning for a walk, but I would rather have gone in the opposite direction toward Telegraph Hill for a look at the view.

We came out of the alley into a small street overhung with

laundry which seemed to be mostly gray and black. All the faces were Chinese, and Lee passed a civil word with some of them. Nobody said a word to me, but then my Chinese isn't that good. A ring of small boys playing marbles on the sidewalk declined to let us through, so we walked in the gutter among the rotten vegetables. Across the street, sober-faced locals listened passively to a strident speech by a hollow-cheeked boy standing on an empty vegetable stand.

"Gabriel Fong," I said as we passed the gathering.

"Pardon me?" said Lee politely.

"Your boss, the man who wouldn't mind if you brought me in dead, is Gabriel Fong. Am I right?"

He might have been about to answer, but just then a prowl car turned onto the street about fifty yards ahead and was closing on us fast. My gut tightened, and I supposed that Lee wasn't exactly indifferent.

"Mr. Goodey," he said calmly, "you may wave to your friends if you like. But if they stop, you're a dead man."

Bearing that well in mind, I let my feet move me along automatically while I watched the squad car come nearer. When it was close enough, I forced my mouth into a broad smile and waved in a subdued but very friendly manner. This may have come as a shock to the two cops in the car, because I soon recognized them as John Barnett and Glynn Mapes, not two of my favorite people on the SFPD. Nor I theirs. Mapes's pointy jaw dropped, and from the corner of my eye I saw John's woolly head whip around. But there was no screech of tires, no shouts, no nothing. Maybe they thought I was drunk.

Perhaps I was walking in a disappointed way, because Lee said: "It won't be long now. Turn into that small opening just past the herb shop on the right." Schooled by nearly twenty years of army and police discipline and a lifetime of cowardice, I did as I was told and found myself in a narrow, high-walled passageway about the width of two bowling alleys. Half a block down at the end of the passage was a dirty green door in a brick wall nearly black with age.

"Straight ahead," said Lee. "Just keep going," he added reassuringly. "There's only one way out of here."

Once inside the green door, Lee said, "All you have to do is keep climbing until I tell you to stop." He was right. The route was clear enough: a thin set of steep and well-worn stairs leading straight up to a small landing. As I climbed I made the mistake of continuing to breathe. The building had the aroma of a linebacker's sweat socks, but it didn't seem to bother Lee, who continued to pad softly behind me. At the landing I paused, but Lee prodded me again, directing me to yet another steep set of stairs.

This time the landing was long, narrow, and murky, and voices were coming from behind a door at the head of the stairs. Keeping the revolver leveled at my chest, Lee darted around me and did a little fancy knuckle-work on the door. With a rustling of chains, the door cracked open, revealing a young, worried-looking Oriental face. Then it opened a lot wider and Lee shoved me into a small room containing half a dozen Chinese youths and someone else I knew.

"Hello, Joe," said Lum Kee. "I've been expecting you."

Lum Kee was sitting at a small table with yet another ledger book open in front of him. He had a smudge of dried ink on his round cheek. Lounging about on hard chairs were the youths. One of them had a new bandage over his left ear. Another had a splint on the middle finger of his right hand. Several others wore attractive facial bruises. None of them said hi.

I did what I could to straighten out my clothing, but I knew I didn't look my best. Lee received a nod of approval and went over to lean against the door and pick his teeth.

"Hello, Lum," I said, trying not to look too surprised. "I

don't want to sound stupid, but are you the someone Lee said wanted to see me?"

"That's right, Joe," he said. "But from the look of your face and clothes, you weren't too eager to come. I hope Lee wasn't too rough with you." He didn't seem all that concerned.

"Oh, no," I said, fingering the lump at the base of my skull. "I was a little reluctant at first, but Lee persuaded me. He's a very persuasive boy. But it wasn't really necessary, Lum. If he'd said it was you, I'd have come without any persuasion at all." I looked at Lee, but he was communing with nature. The Czech popgun was stuck in his waistband.

"Would you, Joe?" Lum Kee asked. "Somehow, I doubt it. I seriously doubt it."

He had me confused there. "What are you talking about, Lum Kee? I know we've never been the best of buddies, but why the hell wouldn't I come see you?"

He gave me a look that would have scared a debtor to death. "You know the answer to that as well as I do, Goodey," he said. "Let's drop all the pretense. Who did you think you were fooling with that silly act of getting kicked off the police force, leaving town, and then suddenly turning up again? I'm not a fool, you know."

I'm afraid I just looked dumb and said: "Act? Lum, you know—"

"I know only that you're getting to be a nuisance, Goodey. You and your fat friend were beginning to—"

"Seymour," I said. I may be a bit slow on the uptake, but nobody has to draw me a picture. "Is that why you had Kroll killed, Lum? Because you thought that he and I were working together and getting too close—too close to something you had going on? Was that it?"

"Your friend was killed," Lum Kee said, eyeing Lee as a teacher looks at the class dunce, "because someone didn't make sure what he was doing before he struck." Lee looked embarrassed.

"Make sure?" I said. "Make sure of whom he knifed? Lum, are you trying to tell me in your obscure way that it was supposed to be me bleeding all over the cheap carpet outside my apartment instead of Seymour Kroll?"

Lum regarded me as if I'd asked him today's price on bean sprouts. "You could say that, Goodey. But believe me, it was nothing personal. I didn't really want to do it." He waved a plump-backed hand near his head like a man warding off mosquitoes. "But these are difficult times for a businessman. Even without the competition I face…"

I cut him off. "Spare me your miseries, Lum. I cry easily. I hate to puncture any illusions you have about my powers of detection, but I haven't the slightest idea what you're talking about. Aside from peddling overpriced Communist-made canned goods, I don't know what you're up to. I always thought you were some sort of crook, but what kind I never knew. And I certainly haven't been investigating you. With Kroll or with anybody else."

Lum looked as though I'd spiked his soy sauce.

I tried to seem sincere. "Have I ever lied to you, Lum? In our long and honorable friendship?" I was pushing it a bit. "Have I ever even been late with the rent?" If I knew my man, that should weigh in my favor.

Lum put on his "credit, yes? credit, no?" face, and I knew I'd have to wait him out.

In the meantime I occupied myself looking over his coven of young thugs and calculating my chances of bulling my way out of there. They didn't look good. One of the lads, the one with the bent ear, caught my roving eye and looked as though he'd like to kick it into the next block. My no-hard-feelings smile didn't have much impact. The rest of them eyed me the way a duck watches a June bug.

Then Lum's voice snatched me back from my reveries of survival. "I think you must be telling the truth, Goodey," he said. "I gave you credit for being much smarter than you really are."

"That's okay." I forgave him. I could see a flickering light at the end of the tunnel. Just barely. "It's a mistake anyone could have made." I pretended to relax, although it probably looked as if I were going to collapse. I asked, "Do you mind if I sit down?"

"No," said Lum absently. "Go ahead." He nodded toward a chair at the side of his desk, and I pulled it toward me. It wasn't much better sitting down. The back of my head still ached, and my face felt as if I'd shaved with a handful of gravel.

Lum Kee interrupted this personal inventory by looking up at me and saying, "Joe, I'm afraid we're going to have to kill you."

20

Lᴜᴍ Kᴇᴇ ꜱᴜʀᴇ ʜᴀᴅ ᴀ ᴡᴀʏ ᴏꜰ ɢᴇᴛᴛɪɴɢ ᴀ ꜰᴇʟʟᴏᴡ'ꜱ attention. He had a hundred percent of mine, anyway.

But what can you say to an announcement like that? "Oh, really?" I couldn't think of a thing to say. Or maybe it was because just at that moment somebody dumped a barrel of sand down my throat. My mouth was drier than a hangman's sense of humor.

Then a strange, high-pitched voice came from somewhere: "Do you—uhhhh—do you think I could have a drink of wa— water?" It must have been me speaking unless the lad behind me was a ventriloquist, a bad ventriloquist. The last word barely squeezed out like the last of the toothpaste, and I knew how the tube felt.

"Of course, Joe," Lum Kee said. He snapped at the boy with the finger in a splint, who quickly left the room. I thought of volunteering to get my own drink. Hell, I'd have gone to get them all a drink. But I sat there waiting—nobody said a word— until there was a cryptic knock on the door, and the boy came back, carrying a bottle of Chinese beer.

Warm Chinese beer. If Lum was trying to weaken my will to live, he was going about it the right way. Chinese beer tastes like Neolithic swamp water. But just then I'd have lapped the dew off the Lone Ranger's saddle. I forced down a long gulp of the beer and showed most of my teeth to Lum Kee.

"That was great," I lied. "Now, what were you saying, Lum?" What the hell, he might rephrase his statement to my advantage. He didn't.

"I really am sorry, Joe," he said somberly, "but you know too much. I don't see how we can let you go now, do you?"

I did, but I think that was a rhetorical question. I gave it a try anyway. "I don't know anything, Lum," I said. "I don't even know what sort of racket you're running. And even if I did, I'm not even interested. I'm not a cop anymore." That was true enough.

"Aren't you, Joe?" Lum Kee peered gravely over his ledger at me. I'll say one thing for him as a villain: he didn't gloat. "Then why did you visit the mayor yesterday? How was it that you were drinking with his brother last night? That doesn't sound like an ex-policeman to me."

"I can explain all that," I said, "if—"

"And besides, there's the death of Seymour Kroll, whom I believe you called Chum. You know how he died."

"It was Chub," I said, "with a b." But he had me there. I did know how Chub died. But only because he had told me.

"Yes, but..."

"And he was your friend," Lum Kee continued. "Certainly you'd have to try to see that his murderer was punished."

Lum Kee had me in a dilemma. How could I disavow Seymour as a friend and pretend not to care whether anybody got done for his murder? Easy. And I was just about to start when Lum rattled off something in Chinese, and I found myself being lifted from the chair by several pairs of willing hands.

"Lum!" I said with a certain amount of alarm. "Lum, can't I..."

"Goodbye, Joe," Lum Kee said, and, believe it or not, he dived back into his ledger. Talk about devotion to business. And I was being propelled toward the door with Lee in front of me, pointing his pistol at my wishbone.

With his eyes still on me, Lee half turned to slip the chain and was opening the door when he was saved the trouble. The door seemed to explode into the room, followed by a mob of Chinese teenagers led by Gabriel Fong. Lum Kee's boys quickly lost interest in me and began trying to fend off the Christian horde. Things got confused in the jammed doorway, what with all the yelling and slamming of fists into faces. So I backed off and looked for someplace a little less busy.

There was an oasis of calm behind Lum Kee's desk, and in the middle of it that successful businessman was reaching deep into a side drawer with an intent look on his face. I went over the top of his desk as his hand came out full of something black and ugly. It was an automatic pistol of some bastard make—probably Japanese or Russian. I don't know what he intended to do with it—perhaps scare us to death—but my kick to his wrist spoiled that plan. I put an arm around his thick neck and started to pull his head off.

He didn't like the idea much. "Stop, Joe Goodey," Lum Kee croaked. "I surrender." I gave his head a couple more twists just for the fun of it.

Things were calming down considerably in the little room. The resistance of Lum Kee's little band had quickly turned into a fight for survival, and Fong's muscular missionaries soon had them driven into a corner.

Fong was in the middle of the room, overseeing surrender

terms. I put a hammerlock on Uncle Lum and was taking him over for a family reunion when a newcomer appeared in the doorway. It was Mickey, the sawed-off kid from my apartment. He was breathing hard, and in his right hand was the longest, sharpest-looking knife I've ever seen. His eyes were bright and glassy.

"Mickey," said Gabriel Fong, moving toward him, "it's all over. We've won." Fong held a gentling hand toward Mickey and toward the knife he held. I wouldn't have done that. But I don't think Mickey even saw him. The boy had his eyes fixed on Lum Kee and was moving toward him—and me. He held the knife at belt level as if he knew what he was doing.

Lum Kee was between me and Mickey, and I was about to do something to change that position when the boy lunged swiftly, and about four inches of the knife went soundlessly into Lum's stomach. I could feel every inch of it.

I let go of Lum Kee, and he brought both fat hands around to grip the blade, to push it away. But by then Mickey had released the handle, and the bloody knife slipped out of the wound and fell to the dirty linoleum. Lum Kee's grasping hands closed over the gushing wound as if to hold in the blood.

"Gabriel," he said. His eyes were on Fong. "Please help me." His face was almost placid, and didn't belong with the words or with the blood, dark and viscous, welling up from under his folded hands, running the obstacle course of his fingers and dripping onto his ancient black trousers. Lum took a step toward his nephew, then stopped. His knees broke in a strange, twisted way, and he fell heavily onto his left shoulder and flopped face down on the grimy floor.

Gabriel Fong, already moving forward, fell on his knees beside his uncle. I was moving toward the desk and the telephone on it. I gave the ambulance service the address, how to get there and the information that we had a heavy bleeder on our hands. When I looked up, Fong was doing a good job of comforting his uncle. Lum Kee lay neatly on the floor with his beetle's eyes open but not looking at anything in particular. The janitor wasn't going to be happy about all that blood on the floor.

"I think he's gone into shock," said Fong, "but his pulse is strong. Is an ambulance on the way?"

I nodded. "Why did he do it?" I asked, shooting a glance at Mickey, who stood crying noisily and being comforted by the other Dragons.

"Fsui-tang died early this morning," Fong said, getting up on one knee, "in a shack out near the Cow Palace where Mickey had taken her from your apartment. I knew he was after my uncle, and that's one of the reasons we invaded this place today. We wanted to stop him. And also because one of the boys saw Lee pick you up this morning. That made it all the more urgent."

"I think so, too," I said. "But why should he want to stab Lum Kee?"

Fong looked down at his wounded uncle and then sadly at me. "I'm afraid, Joe," he said, "that my uncle was the central figure in the ring which has been providing Chinese kids in San Francisco with drugs and exploiting them in many other nasty ways. He has now paid for his crimes."

"He's likely to pay a bit more," I said. "The police are on their way here, too."

As I said this, I was looking around for Lee—my good friend Lee—but I couldn't see him. He wasn't with the cowed remnants of Lum Kee's junior army. For a moment I thought he'd gotten away. But then I saw an arm and a leg sticking out from under the door which had been torn from its hinges in the charge. I flipped the door aside and uncovered Lee, squashed, unconscious, but still breathing. One of the Dragons had the

Czech pistol and was admiring it like a new toy. I reached into Lee's coat pocket and pulled out my service revolver and sap. Putting them where they belonged, I looked over at Fong. He was busy with Uncle Lum. I quietly left the room, heading back toward North Beach.

21

When I got back to Rico's, Irma, naturally enough, was gone. In fact, the whole crowd had changed. Now sitting around Rico's little tables were the we-just-finished-drinking-our-lunch-and-we're-sitting-here-having-a-drink-while-we-wait-to-drink-our-dinner crowd. We exchanged warm stares, and I carried on toward The Jungle.

Nobody was there. By that I mean Irma wasn't there. The day bartender, an obvious student, was leaning over the bar catching up on his required reading. At a corner table, two apprentice Mafiosi shook liar's dice to see who was going to buy the next Bloody Mary. I'd always wanted to see the sort of people who drink in The Jungle on Sunday afternoon.

The bartender said he hadn't seen Irma that day, so I settled onto a bar stool to wait. That's one thing the police force makes you good at—waiting. I can wait with the best of them. But it's thirsty work.

The bartender poured me out a beer and looked me over with scientific detachment. "Your face is bloody," he said.

"It's the altitude. It'd stop if I sat on the floor, but then some drunk would probably step on me. What are you studying?"

"Forensic medicine."

"Oh? Okay, I'll give you a snap quiz. Suppose you were asked to testify in court as to the medical implications of the condition of my face. What would you say?"

The bartender, a thin, bony kid with a Jewish forehead, tugged at his cleft chin for a while and squinted across the bar at me. He asked me to turn to the left and then to the right. "The light's lousy in here," he said, "but I'd say those lesions were caused by scraping against something fairly rough, maybe the pavement. There are no deep cuts and no tissue bruising that matters. The left side was done today, but the right side I'd place between twelve and eighteen hours ago. The bump on your right occipital is pretty new. Caused by a glancing blow from something small and hard but lightly padded." He stood back with a smart-aleck smile of satisfaction. "How did I do?"

"Alpha plus," I said. "You pass the course. But you didn't say that the guy who did it was Chinese."

"It's the light in here," he explained. "Outside in the sunlight I could have told you the province his grandmother came from."

"You'll go far. Can I buy you a drink?"

"Save your money," the student said. "You probably need it more than Fat Phil does."

"I do. Speaking of Phil, have you seen him today?"

"Earlier, yes. But not in the last couple hours. Do you want a prognosis of his chances of reaching his fortieth birthday?"

"No, thanks, I—" Just then a sound, not a big sound, more like a sharp *phoum* or a dull *crack*—I'm not much good at onomatopoeia—came from somewhere over our heads, followed by something that could have been a groan.

"You're back in court," I told the student. "What was that sound?"

"What sound?"

"You flunked," I said, getting off the bar stool. "But you can win back some of my esteem if you'll do me a favor."

"What's that?"

"Look at that clock." The timepiece in question was embedded in the belly of a plastic model of Tina D'Oro in working costume. "If I'm not back sitting on this stool in exactly ten minutes, get some police down here."

"Okay," he said. "But what will I tell them?"

"You won't," I said. "They'll tell you. Remember. Ten minutes. No more."

"Ten minutes," he said a bit doubtfully.

As I suspected, the door leading to the toilets also gave onto the stairs going up to the floors above The Jungle. In a previous incarnation, the building must have been a family house, and these would have been for the servants. The stairs were narrow, dirty and creaked a lot, but they did the job.

They took me up one flight through a peeling, green-painted stairwell. And then another. From the top of the stairs, I could hear that it was all happening on the other side of a door on which someone had had the bad taste to paste a luminous orange star. Even through the door, a strange counterpoint of voices—angry, pleading, desperate—filtered into the hallway.

I tried the knob and found the door unlocked. As I turned the knob, another *crack!* sounded, this time definitely the report of a small-caliber pistol. I pushed in through the doorway with my .38 in my hand.

The scene was not a pretty one. Fat Phil was in one corner of a ticky-tacky overstuffed room, doing his best to hide behind a red-leather pouf. He wasn't succeeding, and two bullet holes in his massive, pink-shirted right side testified to his failure.

The wounds, no larger than cigarette burns, weren't bleeding much, as if Phil's fat weren't so much part of him as a removable blanket of armor.

"Joe," Phil cried when his terror-widened eyes had focused enough to recognize me, "stop her. Save me. She's trying to kill me."

He seemed to be right about that. Standing no more than ten feet away was Irma Springler, holding a tiny .22 caliber automatic as if it were an electric hair dryer. She was standing spraddle-legged with an intent expression on her face and her lower lip caught between her even teeth.

"Go away, Joe," she said without looking at me.

"Joe," said Phil. "Please, Joe." He abandoned the idea of shrinking to fit behind the pouf, cast his eyes in several directions, then compromised by forming a shield of his hands and massive forearms and peering with frightened eyes at his determined huntress. "Joe!" he added in a shriek which climbed until it died as a moan.

"I don't like to be nosy," I said to both of them, "but could somebody tell me what's going on here—except for the obvious, that is?"

"It's none of your business," Irma said, still not looking at me. Her eyes had Phil pinned like a gross butterfly. "Go away."

"Nooooooo!" howled Phil.

"I'd like to, Irma," I said. "I really would. But I've got an uneasy feeling that if I did, you'd go on shooting Phil here. And I wouldn't want you to do that."

"He deserves it," Irma said. "He killed Tina, and I'm going to kill him."

"It's not true, Joe," Phil said. "She's crazy." But somehow the way he said it lacked conviction. A thought came to me.

"Is she, Phil?" I asked. He didn't say anything, just crouched there sweating and bleeding and wishing I'd blow

Irma's head off. I wouldn't have wanted to do that. It was a pretty head. "Tell me something, Phil," I added. "What are you doing up here, up these two flights of steep stairs? I thought your climbing days were over. I thought your heart couldn't handle that sort of exercise anymore. You haven't been faking, have you?"

Phil still didn't say anything. He was doing a damned fine impersonation of someone doing his best to overcome a great handicap and being modest about it.

"Sure, he's faking," said Irma bitterly, "the fat, murdering phony. After you left Rico's, I went to my place and then I remembered what it was that was missing from this room. It was a crazy brass letter opener Tina had—one with a phallic symbol for a handle. Somebody sent it to her for a joke. I came here, and the door was open. Phil was in here rummaging around. He tried to bluff his way out, but I kept him talking. And the more he talked, the more something seemed to be fishy. Then I knew: he'd killed Tina. I knew it, Joe, and I've been trying to get him to admit it. I'll kill him if he doesn't."

"And if he does, Irma?" I asked. "What then?"

I could see that Irma hadn't really explored that possibility. She hadn't had time. She gave it a bit of thought. So did Phil.

"I'll kill him," she said flatly, raising the tiny automatic until it was aimed directly at Phil's sweaty moon face half sheltered behind his hands and arms.

"Don't," he said. "Please, Irma, don't."

"You know, Phil," I said. "I think she really is going to kill you if you don't convince her that you're innocent. That is, if you are innocent. Talk to the lady, Phil."

"Christ," he said, "how can I talk with that gun in my face? I'm afraid to open my mouth."

"He's right," I said. "You could at least lower that popgun a bit, Irma. Phil's not going anywhere. If he ran for it, you could shoot his legs off before he got to the door. Besides, I'm here, and I've got a real gun."

Irma thought it over carefully. Then she lowered the barrel of the .22 until it was aimed at Phil's knees instead of his face.

"That's better," I said. "Now, Phil, you were saying?"

Despite his relief, Phil hadn't lost the look of apprehension which would have wrinkled his brow if he hadn't been so fat. "Could I sit down?" he asked. "My legs are shaking so much I'm going to fall down in a minute."

"Sure," I said. "That is, if it's okay with Irma."

We both looked at Irma, and she gave a cool nod. Phil reached for Tina's padded dressing chair and let his awesome weight down onto it. The chair, unused to such burdens, shuddered delicately.

"You comfy now, Phil?" I asked.

"I don't feel good, Joe," he complained.

"You'll feel better after you start talking."

"I've been shot, Joe," he said, surveying his vast side with apparent detachment. "I'm bleeding. I need a doctor. This isn't fair."

"No, it isn't," I agreed. "But if you don't start saying something, Irma is going to put some more holes in you that a doctor might not be able to do anything about."

"But, Joe..."

"Talk!"

"I didn't kill Tina, Joe," Phil said in a rush. "I—I loved her." He looked down shyly. If you've never seen a 350-pound man look demure, it's a frightening spectacle. But my mother taught me never to laugh at a fat man with two bullet holes, however small, in him. As it turned out, I didn't have to. Irma did it for me. It was a nasty laugh, like somebody ripping up old linoleum, but it expressed our mutual doubt if not a good deal of amusement.

"It's true," Phil insisted, glaring at Irma with such righteousness and indignation that I almost believed him. "I did love her. You don't understand. I made Tina what she was. I took Olga Dombrowitz, just an ordinary North Beach bimbo, not even very young anymore, and I turned her into Tina D'Oro—that was my name, you know; I chose it—the hottest thing in North Beach. Hell, in all of America. I made her a celebrity on network TV. Without me, she'd have been just an aging hooker."

I was watching Irma's face while Phil said all this, and she didn't like it much. She believed it, but she didn't like it. And that last bit about the aging hooker made her blink fast and bite her lip. But she didn't say anything. Somebody had to, so I did.

"So, why did you kill her, Phil?"

"I didn't mean to," he said. "She said she was leaving. Really leaving, this time. Not like all the other times when she was trying to get more money, better billing, a bigger slice of the action. Hell, she owned half of The Jungle as it was."

"Tina *was* The Jungle, you slimy bastard," Irma said, as if coming out of a trance.

"Sure," Phil said, "sure she was The Jungle. Without her, it was just another topless joint. Don't you think I know that? And this time she was really leaving. Some offer from a big hotel in Vegas. 'Tina D'Oro' in neon lights over the Strip. Those magnificent tits I paid for bouncing in some Vegas show bar. She was really going to do it this time. Nothing I said made any difference. She was sitting right in this chair, playing with that stupid letter opener and laughing at me. Telling me how empty The Jungle was going to be after she left. I got mad. I've got feelings, too, you know. I grabbed the letter opener out of her hands, and she tried to get it back. She called me names. She called me some awful names."

Phil ran down like an obscene mechanical toy. He let his

head fall forward and sat slumping in the sleazy, padded chair. Sweat from the top of his head ran down over his vast brow.

"And then what, Phil?" I asked. Irma just stared, her mouth unconsciously hanging open. The .22 hung limply from her hand. I could have taken it away from her. Maybe.

Fat Phil raised his head and looked directly at me. It was as if he had forgotten that Irma and her gun were there.

"I got mad, too," he said. "She was trying to scratch me. I said, 'Take the fucking thing' and I pushed it at her as she was coming toward me. It went in just like cutting butter. Honest to Christ, just like nothing. It went in right between her tits, and she started pumping blood, gallons of it. She was still coming toward me, but I dodged out of her way, and she fell on that big, orange rug I bought her. And she was dead. There was no way I could have stopped that blood. She was dead. Right there. I couldn't believe it. I didn't know what to do."

"You could have called for an ambulance," said Irma in a calm, almost dead voice. "You could have saved her life."

"She was dead, I tell you! She died like that." He tried to snap his sausage fingers, but they slid across each other wetly and noiselessly. As silently, probably, as Tina had died. "Like that."

"And that's how you're going to die, Phil," Irma said, coming to life again and raising the handgun on a level with Phil's head. "Now." I could sense her gathering all her strength to pull the trigger.

"Irma!" I said sharply. "Hold it." She didn't lower the pistol, but she turned her head and lifeless eyes toward me. She said nothing, but I knew she was waiting for what I had to say.

"You don't want to kill him," I said. "It's not worth it. Let the State take care of Fat Phil. With that heart of his, even a manslaughter rap will finish him off. He'll die in jail. If you kill him, you'll be an old, old lady before you see the street again." I was still holding my gun in my hand, but it felt as useless as a steam iron. "My God, Irma, why waste your life on this slug?"

"I have to, Joe," Irma said. "I have to kill him."

Fat Phil was following our dialogue as a tennis fan follows the ball in flight. He was interested. But I think he felt left out too.

"Could someone please get me a doctor?" he said plaintively to nobody in particular. "I'm bleeding." He was hunched over with his chins on his chest and his hand splayed over his right side, trying to cover the two bullet wounds which were still seeping only a little blood.

"For Christ's sake, why, Irma?" I asked. "All right, you were Tina's friend. Maybe you were her only friend. But that's no reason to feel that you've got to take personal revenge on Phil. Do you think you'll feel better if you kill him?"

"No," Irma said, and out of the corner of my eye I could see Phil brighten up as much as a fat man with two bullet holes in him is capable of brightening up. Then Irma continued, "But I've got to do it."

I didn't say anything. I knew there was a reason in there somewhere, and that it would come out by itself. It would have to, or Irma would crack. Then it did.

"Joe," Irma said softly but with great force, "I loved Tina. I loved her. She was my life."

Irma read something into my expression that I didn't know was there yet. Her eyes brightened, and her mouth went firm. "You can scoff if you want to, Joe. I don't expect you to understand." She blinked hard and tossed her head.

"I'm not scoffing, Irma," I said as sincerely as I could. "I'm just a bit—uh—"

"Surprised? Surprised that a woman can love another woman rather than a man? That Tina could prefer me to—to a machismo copper who thinks a woman is just something to push into bed?" That hurt. It really did. I didn't push her.

Irma whipped around to Fat Phil. "Or a fat slob of a flesh peddler who considered Tina just another pair of tits to be sold over the bar like watered whiskey? Who would have been perfectly ready to dump Tina the minute the slobs who come into The Jungle got tired of her. Who couldn't stop selling Tina's body even after he'd killed her. Put her in the ground to rot...to rot."

Irma's voice had gotten shriller and shriller, and her whole body was drawn with tenseness. Her mouth was pulled back in a smile-snarl that wasn't pretty to see. The hand with the gun in it started to rise from the vertical again as if under its own power. She could see nothing but Fat Phil.

The object of her hatred seemed to wake up from a light trance. Phil was shaking his head and mumbling something as if he were talking to himself. In the dead silence of the room, Irma and I strained to hear what he said. Then some words came clear.

"...Christ's sake," Phil was saying, "to think that Tina was a dyke, a fucking bull-dagger. I..."

That was exactly the wrong thing to say at that moment. The words set me in motion, but it was a little too late.

Irma's gun hand sprang up. Instantaneously, the gun rapped, and Phil's right eye was gone. Except for the blood which began to gush from the eye, Phil's face didn't change. It was frozen in an expression of mild wonder, and it would never change again. His body didn't so much slump as settle into itself like a big balloon under a heavy weight. Then Phil toppled forward with a heavy thud onto the bare floorboards and lay unmoving, flat on his bloody face.

Irma moved quickly across the room and emptied the rest of the .22 bullets into the back of Phil's fat, hairy, defenseless neck. It was a waste of bullets. Then she pivoted and threw the gun at my feet.

"You can call the police now," she said. "I'm finished."

"I don't think I'll have to." Heavy footsteps pounded up the old stairs like second-hand thunder. The door buckled at about shoulder height, clung briefly to its catch, and then crashed open, admitting a well-fed young cop who tripped to a stop with his mouth open. Johnny Maher came in after him with a gun in his hand and certain conclusions rapidly forming behind his pale eyes.

"Hi, Johnny," I said. "We were just talking about you." Irma said nothing. I had put my gun away by then, but I'm sure I must have looked suspicious.

"I'll just bet you were," Maher said.

22

Everybody was very happy.

Mayor Kolchik sat in his vast leather chair, beaming like the bride's father at a Polish wedding. In his hand was a glass of the best whiskey the city's money could buy. The Brother, splendid in his Bolivian admiral's uniform, bubbled with bonhomie. He showed me more of his dentist's artistry than I wanted to see. Ralph Lehman had that giddy, hysterical look of a man whose runaway car has just stopped, teetering on the brink of a high cliff. In his mind's eye he was wearing a Hawaiian shirt on the dock in Sausalito, drowning live bait.

I tried to do my share of grinning, but I couldn't help thinking about Irma Springler, just beginning to learn how to be a prisoner. Or about Phil Franks, who'd had to become a corpse without any practice at all. And I couldn't ignore the fact that I hadn't done much to slow down the process. If I'd been willing to shoot Irma—even just a little—he'd still be alive. But I consoled myself that I'd saved the State a tremendous amount of money for his food alone. Irma wouldn't eat nearly as much, or for as long. I'd tried to see Irma in the cells, but she wouldn't see me. The message she sent said that she was going to do it the hard way.

One of the reasons I'd accepted the mayor's invitation to drop by his office was that I thought I'd do what I could to get Irma a break in court. I was biding my time until the right opportunity came up.

"Yessir, Joe," The Brother was saying, "it's all over now. Thanks to you. I have to admit I thought you were a dumb bastard, but you zeroed in where Maher and his jerks failed. Where we all failed," he added, with a fairly meaningful look at Ralph. But Ralph wasn't really there. He should have hung a big sign on his forehead: "Gone Fishing."

"Tell me," Bruno said, "how'd you know that the Springler broad would lead you to Tina's murderer?"

"It's a trade secret, Bruno," I said, tapping the side of my nose. "We private detectives have our little tricks, you know. Just be satisfied that the murder has been solved. Neat, clean, no loose ends. It's buried as deep as Tina D'Oro."

"Deeper," said Bruno with some satisfaction.

"By the way," I said casually, directing my words to the mayor, "what are you going for in the Springler trial? You know she's going to plead guilty."

"Murder One," said The Brother before His Honor could open his mouth. "Murder oh-enn-eee. I'm not settling for less than life, with a mandatory fifteen, maybe twenty. Why, she shot that fat boy down in cold blood. She flat out executed him."

"You're not settling, Bruno?" I said. "Since when are you running the district attorney's office?"

Bruno got that Watch-it-boy-I'm-about-to-get-exercised look on his face. "Listen, Goodey," he said, going cerise around the chops, "you did a damned good job, but if you think..."

"I do think, Bruno," I said. "I think it. You've got what you want, but now you're getting greedy. I'm not going to let you buy Irma a season ticket to Tehachapi just because it makes you feel like a big man and not an overblown property clerk."

Now it was Bruno's turn. "You're not going to let me? How are you going to stop me, Goodey? You've got about as much pull in this town as a busted flush."

"Easy, little brother, easy," I said. "If you try out your running spikes on Irma, all I've got to do is whisper a few sweet nothings to my friends at the *Chronicle*, and you two will be lucky to get berths on the last banana boat back to Poland."

Bruno was up and out of his chair and on his way over to wring my neck when Mayor Kolchik, who'd so far been watching us scuffle like a couple of playground desperadoes, said sharply, "Bruno!" If that was supposed to stop The Brother, it didn't. I was looking around for something to break over his head, when Ralph stuck out a big foot, and Bruno fell like a majestic oak full length on the expensive Oriental carpet. I was up and about to try for the point-after-touchdown with his head when a mighty roar caught my attention.

"Goodey! Stop right there. Sit down!"

Sanford Kolchik was up from his baronial chair with veins like soda straws popping in his thick neck. Bruno, now on his hands and knees, seemed to have been stopped by the bellow, too, so I backed off. But I didn't relax. Bruno thought it over several thousand times, then got up casually from the carpet as if he'd been examining the weave and stomped back to his chair. I'm glad I didn't see the look he gave Ralph.

When we'd all gotten comfy again, the mayor sat down, made a pyramid of his fingers on his spotless blotter and looked at me. "Well, then, Joe," he said, "what do you think would be a proper plea for the State to accept from Miss Springler? I'm assuming you're not asking me to give her a key to the city."

"Not exactly," I said. "I figure voluntary manslaughter

would be all right, if she won't go for a temporary insanity plea. With a recommendation for mercy, of course."

"Mercy?" Bruno went into his geyser act again. "That fucking dyke deserves the same amount of mercy she gave Franks."

"Shut up, Bruno," the mayor said in a quick aside, and Bruno went back to glowering at Lehman. "I don't know about the mercy, Joe," he said. "That might be a bit strong. But I'll tell you what: I think the district attorney will accept voluntary manslaughter with mitigating circumstances, and the prosecutor won't get rabid or talk about long, lonely years in a cell. Is that all right?"

I didn't have to think very hard about that one. It was the best offer Irma was going to get. "You've got a deal," I said. I made a preliminary motion to get up.

"Another thing, Joe," Kolchik said, and I settled down into my chair again. There had to be a catch. "We've got a deal," he said, "and I'll keep my end of it. But this has got to be the end of the Tina business. All right, I was foolish, and I had to bend a few laws to protect myself. But it's all over now. It has to be. I don't want you to think that knowing about me and Tina is your meal ticket for life. Is that understood?"

"It is," I said, and I meant it. "I don't know anything about Tina D'Oro. I never did." Kolchik smiled with satisfaction, but I wasn't finished yet. "But there's one proviso."

The mayor looked at me and let a hood fall over his eyes. "What is it?"

"The same has got to go for your Cousin Stanislaus. I don't want to hear any more about the grievous harm I did to him and the possibility of criminal charges. I'm not overjoyed that I shot him; I wish I hadn't. But it's a closed chapter. A city cop shot him; let the city settle the rap. If I perforate any more of your relations, you've got a squawk coming, but you've had all the mileage you're going to get out of Cousin Stan. Is that agreed?"

"Agreed," said the mayor solemnly. "I don't think that's too much to ask." Just as I got to my feet, he added: "One last thing, Joe. Have you thought about getting your job back in the department? I'm sure Bruno would have no objection," he said without a glance at his brother. "I think we might even be able to manage a set of sergeant's stripes in a couple of months. I don't want you to think I'm an ungrateful man."

Even Lehman had returned from his reverie to listen to this last bit. He was watching me calculatingly, as if trying to guess how much I weighed.

"What do you think of that idea, Ralph?" the mayor asked.

"It sounds good to me, Your Honor," Ralph said, playing it straight. Then he looked at me. "You know, Joe, you've got only five years to go before you could retire. A sergeant gets a fair pension these days. You've already put in a pretty tough fifteen years earning one; you might as well stick around to collect it."

All three of them were watching me. Even Bruno eyed me with fairly restrained malevolence. Maybe, like a small boy who puts a frog on a hot stone, he just wanted to see which way I would jump. So I satisfied his curiosity.

"Thanks very much," I told Kolchik. "I appreciate the offer, but I'm not going to take you up on it." I swiveled toward Lehman. "You were right, Ralph. I don't look like a cop. And I don't feel like one anymore, either. No offense to your proud calling, but you can keep the stripes. In a few years, I'll probably wish I had that pension, but right now I'll settle for my contributions toward it."

"But what are you going to do, Joe?" Ralph asked. I think he honestly wanted to know.

"I've still got that lovely private operative's license you gave me. I think I'll give it a bit of exercise. There are so many bad private detectives in San Francisco already that one more won't hurt."

"Are you sure, Goodey?" the mayor asked. "My offer closes when you walk through that door." He thought I was being stupid. Lehman thought I was being suicidal.

"I'm sure," I said, as if I were.

"All right, then," Kolchik said. "That's settled. But I'm going to give you a going-away present." He jabbed a button on his desk and spoke into his intercom: "Will you send my other visitor in, Dorothy?"

In about fifteen seconds Johnny Maher came through the door like a man walking into a minefield. The polished effect he cultivated was looking a bit thin in spots, but his crease was sharp. Maher raked his eyes across me expressionlessly and stopped in front of the mayor's desk. He could have been facing a firing squad.

"Sergeant Maher," Kolchik said in a carborundum voice, "I called you in here to meet a friend of mine, Mr. Joe Goodey."

Maher expected anything but that. His mouth opened involuntarily, but no sound came out.

"I've just offered Mr. Goodey a job in the police department," the mayor went on. "Your job. And with your stripes to go with it. Luckily for you, Mr. Goodey refused. He prefers to work as a private detective. I want you to know that Mr. Goodey saved your stripes for you. I wanted to take them. Bruno wanted to put you back in uniform. Wasn't that nice of Mr. Goodey?"

Johnny didn't speak. He stood there stiffly. Whatever emotion he was feeling was buried deep.

"Well?" demanded the mayor. "Wasn't it? Don't you want to thank Mr. Goodey?"

Sure he wanted to thank me. Almost as much as he wanted

to swallow his own tongue. To my surprise, I wasn't enjoying this spectacle very much.

"That's okay, Sandy," I said. "The boy is tongue-tied with gratitude. He can thank me later. I've got to go now."

"All right, Joe," Kolchik said, coming around his long desk. He put a thick arm around my shoulders. "Thanks for dropping in. If you feel like sampling a bit more beer, I've got a new batch just coming along. Be ready any time now."

"Thanks, Sandy," I said, hugging him back. I never feel very comfortable hugging men. I looked at the other three, reading various shades of incredulity in their eyes. "I'll be seeing you gentlemen around," I said. I walked through the doorway. As the door closed, I could hear Bruno start in on Maher, and I felt sorry for him.

On the street floor, I bumped into Gabriel Fong as he was getting into the elevator. He backed out hurriedly, and we stood next to a thick marble pillar.

"Hello, Gabe," I said. "How's your uncle?"

"Not well, Joe," he said mournfully. "Complications have set in, and the doctors don't think he'll live to stand trial."

Fong was back in his sincere black suit with the gold cross on his tie, but there was something intangibly different about him. Recent events had rubbed some of the down off him.

"That's too bad, Gabe," I said, "or a good thing, depending on how you look at it. A trial would have been a pretty messy business, what with the death of Fsui-tang and the dope angle."

"The family will be grieved at Uncle's death," Fong said solemnly, "but they will be much relieved if his name is not dragged through the courts and newspaper headlines. We already have much to atone for if we are to hold our heads high again."

"What about you?" I asked. "Are you going home, or will you continue at the Bible College?"

"Neither, Joe," he said. "My uncle is thoroughly penitent and has asked me to take over his business obligations—his legitimate activities only, of course. They will occupy me for some time."

"What about your work with the street kids?" I asked.

"I'll do as much as I can, naturally," Fong said, "but family obligations must come first. There are many ways one can serve God."

"There certainly are. I've got to go, Gabe. See you later."

"Of course," he said. "But one thing quickly while I think of it. I'll be living in my uncle's house, so I won't need to share your apartment anymore, but..."

"But..." I said.

Fong swallowed laboriously, then got his nerve back. "Well, Joe, even a cursory look at my uncle's records shows that he's charging you much too little for that apartment of yours. With those views it should be bringing in much more money. Do you think—do you think that..."

I'm slow, but I got Fong's drift.

"Do I think that perhaps I could move out so that you could fix it up and double the rent? Is that what you want to know?"

Fong nodded nervously.

"No, I don't think it, Gabriel-boy," I said, patting him on the shoulder. "And don't you think it, either. It won't do you any good. You'll only lose sleep."

I smiled sincerely and headed for the parking lot. There was an old Polish gentleman in San Francisco General Hospital who was overdue for a visit.

THE END

BECAUSE REVIEWS ARE CRITICAL IN SPREADING THE WORD about books, please leave a brief review on Amazon if you enjoyed *Goodey's Last Stand*. Thanks.

SIGN-UP FOR THE FREE NEWSLETTER (NO SPAM, NO BS) TO receive updates and exclusive discounts on the latest Charles Alverson books: watchfirepress.com/alverson

BOOK 2: JOE GOODEY RETURNS IN *NOT SLEEPING, JUST Dead*, investigating the death of a young, wealthy girl who allegedly committed suicide. But as Goodey's investigation comes closer to the truth, the killer might not be the only one who wants him dead.

Buy *Not Sleeping, Just Dead* on Amazon at
watchfirepress.com/goodey2

ABOUT THE AUTHOR

Charles Alverson's writing career has spanned over five decades, during which he has written for publications such as *The Wall Street Journal*, *Rolling Stone*, and *HELP! Magazine*. Alverson has written ten novels, two children's books, and helped co-write the screenplays for Terry Gilliam's cult films *Jabberwocky* and *Brazil*.

Alverson currently lives in Serbia, where he has resided with his wife since 1994.

Download Alverson's anthology of short fiction *Ryan's Way & Other Short Stories* when you sign up for his free author newsletter at watchfirepress.com/alverson.

www.ingramcontent.com/pod-product-compliance
Lightning Source LLC
Chambersburg PA
CBHW032117170626
46808CB00006B/1976